Hint of Charm

# Other Books By Lorin Grace

**American Homespun Series**
*Waking Lucy*
*Remembering Anna*
*Reforming Elizabeth*
*Healing Sarah*

**Artists & Billionaires**
*Mending Fences*
*Mending Christmas*
*Mending Walls*
*Mending Images*
*Mending Words*
*Mending Hearts*

**Hastings Security**
*Not the Bodyguard's Baby*
*Not the Bodyguard's Widow*
*Not the Bodyguard's Boss*
*Not the Bodyguard's Princess*
*Not the Bodyguard's Bride*

**Misadventures in Love**
*Miss Guided*
*Miss Oriented*

*A Little Clean Fun*

**Spellbound in Hawthorne**
*(with Maria Hoagland)*
*Taste of Memory*
*Sprinkle of Snow*

# Hint of Charm

Spellbound in Hawthorne Novel #3

# LORIN GRACE
# MARIA HOAGLAND

CURRANT
CREEK PRESS

*P*rince Charming would have not been less if he only possessed a hint of charm.

# CHAPTER 1

On St. Patrick's Day, a single sneeze sent ripples through the town of Hawthorne. It was a well-known fact that, like all permanent residents of Covington House, Liberty Covington had never been sick a day in her life. She'd never had a cold, never experienced an allergy or even a headache. In grade school, a group of boys pooled their lunch money to purchase a can of sneezing powder from an online joke shop. They'd been disappointed to discover it worked on every other sixth-grader in Hawthorne, but not Liberty. So the news of a sneeze on a sunny March morning spread as fast as Paul Revere warning the Minutemen of the redcoats' march.

Holding a tissue in her free hand, Liberty pushed open the door to Hawthorne Herb & Gift Apothecary.

*Achoo!* She sneezed into her elbow, a skill she learned in kindergarten and never needed until now.

An older woman turned from where she'd been arranging glass bottles of tinctures. "Liberty, what is wrong? I've never heard you sneeze in your life."

"Grandma Tansy, I think I have a cold."

"Impossible."

1

"Really? Explain it to my red eyes, runny nose, and head—
*a-achoo!*" Liberty sneezed into a tissue, sure that her head
would pop like a balloon stretched too far. If only she could
curl up in bed and stay there all day.

"My poor girl. How did this happen?" Grandma Tansy
dragged Liberty over to a chair near the counter. She put
her hands on either side of Liberty's face and examined
her, tilting her head this way and that. "You're right. It is
a common cold."

Liberty rubbed her temples. "Make it go away. The
B&B has the biggest week in thirteen years next month
with the reunion, and I have too much to do to prepare. My
head is going to explode. I can't breathe. I can't be sick!"

"Stop overreacting. It is just a cold." Grandma Tansy searched
behind the counter.

"'Just a cold'? I've never felt so awful in my entire life."
Liberty pulled another tissue out of a plastic packet.

"Don't worry. I have something to help you. Is Lisa or
Dean sick?" Grandma Tansy set a bottle on the counter.

"Grandpa is well. Mom has a little sniffle. She laughed,
saying it was the first time in thirty years she's had a cold."

Grandma Tansy frowned and shook her head. "Sore throat
or not?"

"No sore throat. At least I don't think so. It feels weird,
but it doesn't hurt. I've never even had a headache until last
night." The TV commercials weren't exaggerating as much
as she had always thought they had about the degree of
misery a cold could be.

Grandma Tansy put yellow lozenges into a small brown
bag and added two green and lavender bath bombs. She
held the bag out of Liberty's reach. "I don't know if I should
treat your cold or figure out how you caught one."

"Please? I need to function. You know how important the
reunion is to me and to the town. I have every room filled

2

and have planned more cot beds than the fire chief will probably allow. Plus, there are all the events to finish details on." Liberty hoped Grandma Tansy would feel a bit of guilt since she'd roped Liberty into being on the committee.

"Take the lozenges whenever you feel you need one. They'll clear your head and calm the headache. Tonight, soak in a hot bath with one of these bath bombs, then go to bed. Drink plenty of liquid. And none of your hawthorn berry tea. I'm not sure how it will interact with these."

"The tea doesn't taste right, anyway. It must be my plugged-up nose." Thanks to a web search, she'd discovered that some people reported changes in taste and smell with a cold.

"Colds can do that. $17.75." Grandma Tansy handed Liberty the products as Liberty ran her card through the reader. "Get well soon."

*Achoo!* When Liberty opened her eyes after her sneeze, Grandma Tansy was gone. Liberty didn't have time to ponder Grandma Tansy's vanishing act. She needed to get back to the B&B to meet with the fire chief about the seating capacity for the ballroom and maximum occupants per room.

Liberty popped a lozenge into her mouth. In the few seconds it took to walk to the corner of the block, the soothing effects calmed her headache. She climbed onto the old blue three-wheeled bike. She would have preferred her regular bicycle, but she'd needed the large basket space of Grandpa's adult tricycle. Earlier that morning, she'd dropped the van at Bob's Brakes for a tune-up but couldn't put off her errands for when she had a running vehicle. In thirty days, over five hundred Covington women and girls would descend upon Hawthorne for the fourteenth reunion of the Daughters of Lavinia Hawthorne-Covington Reunion, and everything needed to be ready. That included the van which had seen more miles than most cars.

Another sneeze rocked her body. Grandma Tansy's remedy needed to work faster. Right now, she felt as miserable as every commercial actress who'd ever peddled an over-the-counter cold cure. Liberty checked her errand list before pulling the too-large tricycle onto the street. Only two errands left before she needed to return to the B&B for her meeting with the fire chief: drop off the program file to the printer and pick up eggs from the organic farm as her henhouse was still empty.

Renting a convertible may have been more ostentatious than his uncle had advised, but the opportunity to drive America's rural roads with the top down had Oliver Brad-ford taking chances. He meandered down tree-lined byways in what his grandfather still referred to as the colonies. Somewhere among the suburbs of Boston, he would find the perfect spot for the newest Bradford-Stone hotel and get back into Uncle Pierceton's good graces.

Tiny new light-green leaves covered a few trees. Occasionally a tree hinted at the pink blossoms that would soon be in full bloom. Oliver expected New England to be smoggier, like LA. Some towns he drove through reminded him of those he visited in parts of England while on holiday, only with newer buildings. One could hardly call the landmarks he passed—built in the 1600s—old. But the mix of the old and the new was similar. His Leeds flat was a fairly modern chrome-and-glass affair similar to the Boston hotel he stayed in the night before.

A large building caught his notice, and Oliver's eyes moved off the road. A honk from the oncoming car alerted him to the fact that he'd wandered onto the left side of the road instead of the right. Being aware of driving on the wrong side of the road had been one of the last warnings his assistant had given him before Oliver had flown to the States yesterday. How difficult could it be? The steering wheel was on the wrong side of the car. Oliver vowed to pay more attention.

A green road sign announced that taking a left at the next cross street led to the town of Hawthorne.

Although he hadn't intended to visit Hawthorne so early in his tour of the area, his curiosity got the best of him. The law firm that Bradford-Stone Worldwide had contracted previously to conduct a search for a location for the hotel had been less than forthcoming in their choice of Hawthorne for a hotel location. During conversations with the Hawthorne city planner, Oliver had gotten the distinct impression that not only was a hotel not needed, it would be unwanted because the hotel chain was British—a sentiment that didn't fit with the interactions he'd had with other American ventures.

The town didn't look much different from a half dozen others he'd driven through that day. His grandmother would have dubbed it "charming." Mid-nineteenth-century architecture dominated the downtown areas, sprinkled with homes dating to the early eighteenth century, and here and there, a building from the first half of the twentieth century. Many of the buildings constructed in the past fifty years called upon older architectural styles to blend in. A boxy white church bordering one side of a park reminded him of photos he'd seen on almost every New England tourism website.

He recognized the bronze statue of the female Revolutionary War hero from one of the websites he'd used to research the town after the hotel deal fell apart. It was one of those puffed-up American stories where the sixteen-year-old girl warned the revolutionaries of the British marching on Concord. The fantastical portion of the story was that she supposedly stopped the King's forces from reaching Concord by means of magic that created a dense fog.

He turned left to circle the block that, as Acquisitions Vice President, he had been persuaded to purchase. It was well situated, but he could see why the townspeople hadn't wished for a hotel to be built on a block home to so many small businesses and so near the heart of the town.

Bradford-Stone Worldwide had lost half a million pounds on the venture. Half a million pounds that had him driving around Massachusetts, finding a more suitable hotel location or being permanently demoted.

Completing the circle of the block, Oliver had seen enough. Through his own inattentiveness, Wendall A. Smith, former attorney, had duped him. The Miami and Caribbean hotel projects had been so much more interesting that he hadn't checked and double-checked the information he'd received as he should have. As a result, his uncle had asked Oliver to travel to Hawthorne and apologize personally to the affected building and business owners. Oliver hoped to work with the director of the city's chamber to do it in a group setting to make the apologies quick and painless.

He passed the statue again and followed a sign for the next town. He passed a large house with a tasteful sign proclaiming it Covington House Bed & Breakfast. Three trees bloomed in the palest of pink buds. He slowed to look at them.

Someone shouted.

Oliver tried to swerve, but there was no way he could avoid hitting the woman on the giant tricycle in his lane.

# CHAPTER 2

Under her bike helmet, the headache Liberty had been fighting all day quadrupled in size. Mud and something gooey covered her cheek; she hoped it wasn't blood. She turned her head. Eggs. Broken eggs and yellow yokes surrounded her. Six dozen of Hill Farm's finest organic eggs. Liberty tried to push herself up but was trapped by the frame of the bike, her foot caught in the pedal strap. Pain shot through her shoulder.

"Hold still. I'll move your bicycle." The accented male voice cut through her foggy thoughts.

"Stop! Don't move her." The pounding of feet on the pavement signaled others joining them.

Liberty turned her head to get a look at the approaching men, and pain ripped through her shoulder. She laid her head back on the ground and waited for them to come into view. The fire chief and a police officer slowed as they reached her. The meeting with the fire chief. Not a good way to start the inspection. Late, covered in eggs, and laying in a ditch.

"The ambulance is on its way." The fire chief knelt next to Liberty's head. "Where do you hurt?"

"Liberty Belle?" From the other side of the rock wall, she heard Grandpa's voice.

"He was in my lane." Liberty voiced the last thought she'd had before she attempted to swerve to avoid the convertible careening toward her.

"Officer Hastings is taking care of that. Where do you hurt?"

"Greg?" She searched for the officer. Greg Hastings was one of Liberty's oldest friends. In high school, she would have been embarrassed for him to see her in such a state. Now, not so much, he'd seen her in worse situations, like when their team lost the Fourth of July tug-o-war.

His voice answered from behind her. "I'm here, Libs. Tell the chief where you hurt so we don't injure you more getting you out from under this trike."

"My head, shoulder. *Achoo.*" Automatically Liberty brought her hand up to cover her sneeze and ended up covering her face with egg goo.

Sirens wailed.

"Does your foot or ankle hurt?"

Liberty tried to wipe the goo off her face.

"Here. Use my handkerchief." The accented voice again. Not East Boston like she'd first thought. Her brain couldn't place it.

Greg caught the cloth before Liberty could. "Miss Independence, I can see you are in pain."

"Greg, I—"

"Allow others to help you now and then." With professional detachment, he wiped the egg from her face.

The fire chief waited until her vision was clear. "Ankle—does it hurt?"

Oops, she hadn't answered. "No, my ankle doesn't hurt."

More feet pounded on the pavement. "The EMTs are here." Greg lightly touched her back. "I'm going to move and let them in here. I'll be around later to discuss your sneeze." Of course he focused on the sneeze; he'd been the boy who helped buy the joke powder in grade school.

Until the weight of the bike was gone, she hadn't realized her leg had been pinned. Apparently, she'd lied—her ankle hurt as well as her hip. However, compared to her shoulder, neither pain was significant.

"My shoulder." She reached for her right shoulder, but one of the EMTs beat her to it. His gentle touch sent a jolt of pain through her, and she yelped.

The other EMT asked tons of annoying questions, including who the president of the United States was, today's date, and a list of things she was to remember and repeat.

"Apple, pencil, zebra." The list wasn't hard to remember.

He shined a light in her eyes. "I think you should go to the emergency room, miss."

"I don't have time — I need to get more eggs."

"Liberty Belle," Grandpa's voice carried a warning edge to it. "Go to the hospital. Don't worry about the eggs."

An EMT removed her helmet. A large chunk of the plastic frame dangled from the strap. Her head must have hit the stone wall that separated the road from Covington House. Thank goodness she promised her father she would always wear a helmet when she rode a bike. Twenty years later, the promise paid off.

"That could have been your brain." Mom's voice came from behind her.

Liberty wasn't sure when her mother joined Grandpa.

"Lisa, don't fret, she'll be fine."

From where she lay Liberty couldn't see her grandfather comforting her mother, but she knew his arm would be around Mom.

Pain shot from her neck through her shoulder. Liberty clenched her teeth to keep from yelling again. The EMTs gave directions and immobilized her neck. They rolled her

9

onto a backboard, and Liberty got her first look around that didn't include the ditch.

On the other side of the rock wall, her mother stood with one of her everything-will-be-fine smiles plastered under worried eyes. Grandpa's face was unreadable. Greg Hastings stood next to a red convertible with a man dressed in a tweed jacket over a sweater. The unusual combination was decidedly not local. And neither was he. He wasn't as tall as Greg, which meant under six feet.

"I'm terribly sorry. T'was all my fault." His accent was too distinct to miss now. Greg had better throw the book at the driver.

"You're British." She, Liberty Belle Covington, had been felled by a Brit!

Americans always pointed out the obvious when Oliver spoke. Usually, when a woman told him he was from England, it was followed by flirtation. However, the woman with the short blond hair said it as if it was an accusation.

"I suppose you forgot we drive on the right side, as in, the correct side of the road here."

"Liberty." The police officer taking down his information called the woman's name. "This isn't a reenactment. Be nice."

She made a face at the officer. It could have been pain-induced, but Oliver doubted it. American police officers were nicer than he expected from TV.

An EMT joined them. "Are you injured?"

Oliver held up his hands. "Only my wrist. From the airbag, I assume."

"Hm. It doesn't look like a chemical burn. The newer car airbag systems shouldn't do that." With gloved hands, the

EMT probed his wrist. "There is some swelling. You should get it x-rayed. There is room in the back of the ambulance."

"What about my car?"

"They will tow it to Bob's. Unless you have other arrangements," said the officer.

"I'm not sure. It's a rental." How did rental companies deal with automobile accidents in the States? Or medical billing? He'd heard stories about navigating the American healthcare system. Presumably, someone in Bradford-Stone's HR department could help with that. Technically, this was work related. How did he go about paying for the woman's medical bills? None of these questions had come up in his previous visits to the States.

"Your car is probably covered. This ticket won't be." The officer handed Oliver a paper. "You should contact the rental car company to report the accident as soon as possible. They'll need this information for the accident report."

"Thank you." Oliver tucked the papers into his wallet.

The EMT gestured to the waiting ambulance. "This way, sir."

As Oliver sat on the bench, Liberty's eyes met his. Oliver always hated the term *expressive eyes* because everyone's eyes expressed something, even if it was a void of emotion. The accusatory glare Liberty leveled at him would have been deadly in an alternate world where superheroes existed. From earlier observation, he doubted she hid her emotions.

The ambulance doors slammed behind him. The sirens were not as loud inside the ambulance as he'd expected. Oliver pushed the odd thought away and turned to Liberty. "In answer to your earlier question, I am aware I should have been driving on the right side of the road. I'm afraid I was distracted by the most spectacular tree. It's the only one I've seen blooming."

She opened her mouth and then shut it again with the oddest look on her face. She sneezed into the inside of the elbow, explaining the expression.

The EMT paused his work and stared at her. "It's true? You got a cold?"

"Yes, Eric, I can sneeze. I'm surprised you didn't compare notes with Greg."

"I'll make sure the ER docs check that out. Liberty Covington having a cold is the most spectacular thing to happen on a call yet this week." The EMT didn't seem to joke. If she'd never had a cold in her life, wouldn't that make it some sort of record?

"Ha, ha. I can't be the only twenty-four-year-old who's never had a cold before." She rolled her eyes. Halfway through, she noticed Oliver watching her, and the smiling response to the EMT's teasing faded. Oliver braced for another glare, but she turned her face away for the rest of the ride.

At the hospital, he was put in a separate curtained cubical.

After an X-ray and a bag of ice, Oliver was handed a stack of papers and asked to sign on an electronic tablet. On the other side of the curtain, voices escalated.

"Broken? What do you mean broken?"

The doctor's voice didn't carry as well as Liberty's. Oliver assumed the answer was obvious.

"I can't wear a sling for six weeks. I have too much work to do." Her comment was punctuated with a sneeze and a whimper.

A nurse came into Oliver's curtained cubicle, interrupting his eavesdropping. "You are free to leave, Mr. Bradford. I'll show you out."

Where exactly could he go? In the lobby, he looked for a corner to make some phone calls. The older gentleman who'd been at the scene of the accident sat in a corner. He waved Oliver over. There wasn't a good way to avoid the man whom Oliver assumed was Liberty's grandfather.

"You seem a bit lost." The man nodded at the seat opposite him.

"I am. I've never hit a person before. I'm not sure what to do or where to go now."

"Where were you heading before the accident?"

"I'm not sure."

The old man shook his head. "No wonder you don't know where to go. Do you have a hotel room?"

"I checked out from one in Boston this morning. I figured I'd find someplace tonight."

"We have rooms open at the B&B. More comfortable than one of those generic hotel chains. Give yourself a day or two to recover."

"No offense, Mr.—?"

"Covington. Dean Covington." The man extended his hand in greeting.

Oliver recognized the surname from his research. The inn with that name had been the only competition to the proposed Bradford-Stone hotel. Staying in Hawthorne wasn't a good idea.

They shook hands. "Oliver Bradford. Thank you for your offer, but I don't think your granddaughter would appreciate me staying there since I hit her."

"She welcomes all paying customers, and I'm forcing her to take the next few days off. She won't even know you're there."

"I hit her. Wouldn't that be awkward for you?"

"Accidents happen."

Oliver needed a polite exit. "I need to check on the car."

Dean opened his wallet. "Here's a card for Bob's Brakes. Give her a call. And here is a card for the B&B. I'll hold the Lafayette suite until tomorrow for you. The view is—"

"Mr. Dean Covington?" A man dressed in scrubs stopped near them.

"That's me," said Dean.

"Will you come with me, please?"

Oliver was left alone in the waiting room. His first call was to the car rental agency.

# CHAPTER 3

*L*isa hovered near the bathroom door. "You're sure you don't need help with your hair?"

"Mom… I can wash my hair with one hand." Another advantage of keeping a short hairstyle. "I'm only going to rinse off, then take a bath with those bombs Aunt Tansy told me to use." Or rather, the powder that once had been bath bombs. They'd suffered more damage than she had from the accident.

"I'll bring up some of your hawthorn berry tea."

Liberty started to shake her head before remembering the pain the action would cause. "Tansy told me not to have any while I take her cold cure."

"Just as well. I think this last batch I drank was off somehow. But it might be my nose being stuffed up."

Her mother closed the bathroom door, leaving Liberty to enjoy some rare quiet time. On the way home from the hospital, Grandpa had been insistent that she not step foot in the public areas of Covington House for three days, and the large commercial kitchen was off-limits. Under the influence of a prescription painkiller, Liberty agreed—mostly because it hurt her head to argue.

While she soaked, she listened to her voicemail messages. Her favorite cousin and best friend Makenna had left several.

"Grandma Tansy was by. She said you had a cold. Is that true, or is she having another one of her moments?"

"Walter came over from the café, and he said you were hit by a car?! Call me."

"It is 'gossip about Liberty' day in my shop. Someone posted on the Heard in Hawthorne webpage that you were hit by a Brit driving on the wrong side of the road. Also, the Brit is supposed to be dreamy and have the best accent—not that you'd be impressed. Call me."

Liberty set the phone on the stool next to the tub and called Makenna. "Hey, are you still working?"

"Painting some furniture. I have you on speakerphone, and Quin is here."

Liberty appreciated the warning. "Hi, Quin."

"Hey, Liberty. Get well soon, and let me know if I can do anything. I'm going to duck out so you two can have a private talk."

Liberty ignored the unmistakable sound of a kiss between Makenna and her fiancé.

"He's gone. Tell me everything."

"I have a cold and a broken collarbone. And have ingested more drugs in the last twenty-four hours than I have in my entire life."

"Broken collar bone? Isn't that the one they don't cast?"

"Yup. Sling for six weeks. I don't know how I can get everything done. I had my entire schedule worked out so I would be ready for the reunion."

"Hire some help."

"But I only need temps."

"You know the Monroe twins who work for me. They're looking for more hours; they have big plans for prom. They're both great workers."

"That might help for some of the preparation." There were a few things she could trust to someone else, but most things were up to her. "How am I ever going to convince Grandpa I can run this place if I can't get it ready for the reunion?"

Makenna sighed. "This is going to sound hypocritical coming from me, but you need to learn how to manage others, not run everything all the time on your own. Miss Independence isn't your nickname because July Fourth is your favorite, it's that you do everything yourself."

"Not fair. Only Greg calls me that because he's teasing me about the Miss Hawthorne pageant I lost. Besides, I hired extra help for the summer, including Fiona to cook so that mom and I aren't doing all the things."

"You're still working fifteen-hour days. When is the last time you took a full day off?"

There wasn't a suitable answer. "I can't believe you, the queen of staying-up-all-night-to-work, are lecturing me."

Makenna laughed. "Hello, Pot. It's me, Kettle."

"At least your hard work is getting you somewhere. The B&B isn't filling as much as it was three years ago. Another year like the last, and there won't be one. I can't afford to hire more people."

"Are you sure? You said that last year too, and it turned out to be a good year."

Liberty sighed. Her glass-half-empty projections from last year hadn't come to fruition. "We had a good year, and the reunion will help this one. There are a handful of summer reservations from Covington descendants that are coming to seek their roots this summer. However, the costs keep rising, and it's hard to compete with everyone and their pet penguin renting out a spare room on the internet."

"We'll figure something out."

"That's easy for you to say. You found your magic and got your business going in a new direction, all in the past year.

Not to mention that rock on your finger. Not that I'm ready to get married or anything. I just want…" Liberty trailed off. "Never mind that last thought, it's the pain reliever talking." Liberty rarely talked about her dating life. Even if she had a boyfriend, she wouldn't ever have time to see him. The silly wish she'd made years ago to marry her best friend had backfired repeatedly. The caveat to the wish had been that she'd marry a prince who knocked her off her feet. That was unlikely to happen. Someplace, there was probably a minor prince, but according to the internet, all the princes of marriageable age were taken. Liberty sneezed. "I decided I hate colds."

"So does everyone else. That is so weird that you caught one. The last time a resident of Covington House was sick was like never. I double-checked in my newest histories." Makenna's knowledge of local history surpassed that of the matrons of the Hawthorne Historical Society.

"I'm sure not every cold gets recorded."

"Ask Uncle Dean. He's never been sick, either. As long as someone is living in—not visiting the house—they don't get sick. There isn't a single exception I can find."

"You know how crazy that sounds?" asked Liberty.

"Think about it. We broke into the well thirteen years ago because we thought the water was magic. What if it really is?"

"So the water keeps us from getting sick?"

"No clue. Grandma Tansy was more curious about how you caught a cold than how you could fix it. Maybe she knows something." Makenna had taken to writing down some of the odder things Grandma Tansy had done over the last several months, including shoplifting.

"The way she's been these last few months, I don't know if I trust her." Liberty ran her hand through the pale lavender water. "Speaking of—how do I even know she sold me the right stuff to help with my cold?"

18

"Lavender and green bath bombs?"

"Yes, and some yellow lozenges."

"Sounds right to me. I love those bath bombs. Are you getting sleepy?"

"Yes, but it could be the pain meds."

"Lean back and relax. When the water cools, go to bed. You'll feel so much better in the morning. I'll talk to you then. Good night." Makenna disconnected the call.

Liberty sank lower into the tub, hoping to relieve the pain in her shoulder with the soothing water. The bathwater wasn't from the old well. Only one of the kitchen faucets was connected to the well. Everything else was municipal, including the bathtub's water. Could there be something wrong with the well? The cap hadn't been off since the well was sealed thirteen years ago. How would she even find out? Eventually, the water cooled and Liberty went to bed.

Understandably, the rental company refused to rent a new car to Oliver. Bob turned out to be the exact opposite of the burly tattooed man he'd envisioned when the ride share dropped him off at Bob's Brakes. Bob, full name Robyn, offered Oliver and his suitcases a ride to Covington House B&B. He'd tried calling a larger hotel in Waltham, but they were full. Oliver accepted the ride. At this point, he didn't care where he landed, as long as the room was clean and the bed comfortable.

Dean Covington was at the front desk. "I'm glad you chose to stay with us."

Not much choice to make. Fate decided that he needed to stay near the scene of the crime.

Dean gave Oliver an old-fashioned key and sent him up the wide stairs to room three. Under the number on the door was a brass plate with the word "Lafayette." The other doors had names on them too. The room was larger than he'd expected, with a sitting area as well as a king bed. The furniture and décor pieces were all antiques or replicas. The wallpaper pattern was in the greens and creams of a bygone era. The chances that another room in the B&B looked identical were fairly low.

An oil painting in the sitting area caught his attention. A brass plate read: "*Lavinia confounds the British* by Celie Covington 1875." A woman stood on a hill, her arm raised, tossing something into the wind. Below her, a regiment of redcoats marched into a dense fog. Had they put him in this room to remind him of the story, or did all rooms at Covington house tell something of the folklore behind the family? Someone had rewired the period lamp at the desk to provide for two USB ports, with an extra outlet at the base.

Oliver sat in the large wingback chair and made the call he'd been dreading. "Good Evening Uncle Pierceton."

"Reporting already?"

"Not exactly. I had a slight mishap today." Oliver described the car accident, the steps he'd taken to make sure the woman he'd hit was taken care of, and the lack of a rental car. He didn't mention that he was still in Hawthorne, staying in a room less than seventy meters from the site of the accident.

As he'd predicted, his uncle did not take the news well. "Will you never learn to be responsible? The first day, and you hit someone. I am finding you a driver!"

Oliver patiently listened to the lecture. It wasn't like he'd meant to drive dangerously. Driving on the left side of the road was habit and drifting in that direction just happened. Not an adequate defense. To end his uncle's rant, Oliver promised to pay for the entire thing, using his own money.

"You realize I would fire any other employee over this? What am I to do with you?"

Any other employee would have been fired over the incident with the Hawthorne hotel. The problem was Oliver wasn't any other employee. He was the heir to his grandfather's barony, and short of committing a crime against the crown, Oliver wouldn't be fired from the title. Honestly, he wasn't trying to take advantage of that—well, not anymore. Admittedly, he'd taken advantage of his inheritance during his college days, and Grandfather had dismissed Oliver's indiscretions, as he always had. Only Uncle Pierceton ever held Oliver accountable. Oliver wondered more than once if his uncle didn't deserve the title more than Oliver would. "Honestly, I was trying to be more responsible."

The silence on the other end of the line was full of unspoken words.

"I'm very sorry."

"You always are. Please, get this job right. When you do take over the company, you will need the respect of your employees." A point Uncle Pierceton mentioned often as of late.

"I will. Goodnight." Oliver wasn't sure he wanted to take over so much responsibility. What if he kept making poor decisions? Thousands of jobs would be in his hands. Until the Hawthorne hotel debacle, none of his choices had really mattered—a hotel here, an extended stay there, a resort someplace sunny. Until a woman was almost killed because Oliver trusted the wrong person.

Oliver set up his laptop to check local dining options. There were a few places that looked to be within walking distance, however, it had started to rain, and Oliver would rather not get soaked. He searched for someplace that delivered and ordered Chinese. He recognized the name of the restaurant from the list of owners that he needed to apologize to. As long as he was stuck in Hawthorne, he may as well start the in-person apologies. He drafted an email to Ms. Conley and Mr. Kayhill, the director of the Hawthorne chamber of commerce while he waited for his food. An apology couldn't get much more painful or embarrassing than the one he'd had to make today because of his inattentive driving.

# CHAPTER 1

By 8:20 a.m., Liberty was bored out of her mind. Did people really watch morning news shows? The weather would come in handy, but knowing that the traffic on the tollway or the 90 was backed up as per usual probably didn't help the average commuter much. As for the news, couldn't there be something about puppies? Liberty turned off the TV and paced her room. She paused in front of her dresser. When was the last time she'd dusted in here? All the other rooms in the B&B got a daily wipe down. She'd neglected her own room. She could dust with her left hand.

Liberty went in search of a microfiber cloth. Thanks to some creative additions in the mid-1800s, the best way to the second-floor linen room of the B&B from the family quarters was to walk downstairs through the kitchen and back up a different stairway. There was a way through the attic of the family wing into room six through a three-foot-high wall panel, but Liberty hadn't used that since she was ten and Grandpa caught her in the passage and nailed the secret door shut.

Liberty crossed the hall near the kitchen as the new cook sang off-key to the radio. She hoped the sound didn't carry

23

into the dining area. She hurried up the back stairs, hoping to avoid her mother and grandfather. The door to the service closet stood ajar. Liberty ducked in and snatched a clean yellow dust cloth from the top of the stack behind the door. Out of habit, she checked the supplies to make sure that nothing was running low.

Someone tapped on the closet door. No one ever did that. Liberty opened the closet door farther but couldn't see the person who knocked.

"Pardon me. Would it be possible to get another towel?"

That voice. That accent. It couldn't be the same man from yesterday. No way would he have stayed here after running her off the road. Liberty looked around the door. It was him.

"Sorry, I thought you were housekeeping. I'll go ask at the desk."

"No need." Liberty stepped back into the closet. Her hand hovered over a stack of clean towels. On the shelf below was a stack of retired towels used for cleaning and other emergencies. Most of them had holes or nasty stains. She grabbed a towel from the lower stack. "Here you go."

The towel fell open. There was a baseball-sized hole through the center, which he thrust his hand through. "Thank you." He turned and took several steps away.

This was not who she was. Liberty whirled and grabbed a towel off the top stack. "Wait." She hurried down the hall after him. "I'm sorry, I gave you a towel off the wrong shelf."

"After yesterday, I deserve worse than a towel full of holes."

"You are a guest at our B&B. I have no right to take my anger out on you."

He nodded to her sling. "How much damage did I do?"

Instead of grating on her ears, his accent was soothing. No wonder her cousins thought she was crazy for not liking anything British. Totally not fair. It no longer mattered that this Brit had run her over because he couldn't drive on the right side of the road. "Broken collarbone. The doctor says at least six weeks of recovery. It couldn't have happened at a worse time."

"I don't suppose these things ever happen at a good time."

"Our town's biggest week in thirteen years is only thirty days away. I have so much to do to prepare Covington House for all the visitors." According to Mom, the Brit—whose name she refused to acknowledge—had settled her hospital bill and covered all her future medical expenses relating to the accident. That wouldn't help with the work she couldn't get done.

"Thirteen years?"

"Every thirteen years the female descendants of Lavinia Hawthorne Covington have a massive family reunion of sorts. Women come from all over the country. There probably won't be a hotel available within a fifteen-mile radius of town. The descendants who live in the area offer their spare rooms and guest rooms to cousins they haven't seen for years." The reunion was going to be her time to shine, to prove to Grandpa once and for all that she was worthy to inherit and run Covington House Bed & Breakfast. Now she wouldn't be able to do even half of the things on her list.

"Is there anything I can do to help?"

*No, go away.* "I'm sure you're here on vacation or some such. I couldn't trouble you with that."

"I'm here on business. Unfortunately, I have lost my means of transportation, and my company has revoked my driving privileges."

Liberty bit her lip to hold in a snarky comment. One of the first rules of hosting a B&B was to never offend the guests. She'd already broken that once today.

"You can laugh. That sling gives you the right to laugh all you want to."

Instead, Liberty used her helpful-front-desk voice. "Fortunately, there's ride share, and Massachusetts has a lot of public transportation. Do you need a map?"

"I've been looking at the map of the MBTA trains and subways. I think riding them would actually help most with my research."

"What kind of research are you doing?" Rats. She didn't need to know. Liberty blamed it on his accent, like warm tea for the soul. Seriously, she needed to end the prescription pain meds.

For a moment, his face froze. "You'll hear eventually anyway. I'm looking for a place to put a new hotel."

"Hawthorne does not need a hotel."

"So I have learned." The corner of his mouth tilted up as if there was something funny about the situation.

Filtered stories from her cousin Makenna's troubles during the winter came to mind. "Are you with the company that tried to buy the block downtown?"

"Yes."

This could not be happening. Not only had she been hit by a Brit, but he was also the same one who'd tried to destroy the heart of Hawthorne. If she spent one more moment with him, she would slap him.

"If you'll excuse me, I need to—" Liberty held up the dust cloth and made a hasty retreat. She needed to stay away, far away from him or Grandpa would give her the same lecture he had when she was nine and told some guests they smelled funny. That would not help in her plans to inherit Covington House. For the sake of the B&B, she could be polite to any guest. Even a Brit.

Oliver thought about chasing after Liberty, but the flash of lightning he saw in her eyes before she retreated down the stairs was enough to tell him that doing so would not make things better. He returned to his room with both the ratty towel and the fresh one. She hadn't given him the old one by accident. Obviously, she was a professional and hadn't been able to treat even him poorly as a guest. More than one hotel employee had lost their job with Bradford-Stone for pettiness. Oliver had to admire her quick change of heart. If the hardness in her eyes hadn't given her away, he would never have realized that Liberty Covington considered him to be an enemy.

Not that he could blame her since he was the source of her current pain and problems. Oliver didn't like himself much either at the moment. There had to be something that he, or at least his money, could do. Making sure he paid the medical bills over what the insurance would cover was not much compensation.

He hadn't lied about looking at the Massachusetts Bay Transit Authority public transportation maps, though he'd been trying to figure out how to escape Hawthorne for a more central location rather than work-related research.

Most Americans seemed to do their touring by car, whereas foreign visitors were limited to group tours or what they could easily get to on public transportation if they were unwilling to drive in Boston traffic. With that bit of information in mind, perhaps exploring the Massachusetts transit system would give him ideas for a suitable hotel location. The nearest train station was less than a mile away from the B&B. There was no time like the present to explore, especially when he was quite sure that the hostess of the bed-and-breakfast would like nothing more than to toss him out on his ear.

Checking the weather app on his phone, Oliver grabbed an umbrella and headed out. It wasn't raining yet, but he expected it to before long. Instead of turning south at the first cross street to go to the train station, he continued into the heart of town. He circled the block that he'd driven around the day before. How had he ever been duped into thinking this would be a suitable spot for a hotel? The access was difficult and the parking non-existent. The only thing to recommend the space on the polygonal block was the view of the town's park.

He'd been told he could get the land easy and had believed his source. A source who now sat in the state penitentiary. His uncle had not been pleased. Oliver had since studied a map of Hawthorne. The chamber of commerce was only half a block away. Although he'd intended to do his apology later in the trip, after yesterday's accident, getting the groveling over with as soon as possible might help him get back into his uncle's good graces and back to the office in Leeds.

Oliver crossed the street and passed the bookstore and a café before coming to the Hawthorne Chamber of Commerce. The office was small, and a receptionist sat at the desk. "Is Quinton Kayhill in?"

"Do you have an appointment?" She glanced at her computer. She had to know he didn't.

"No, but can I make one?"

"Let me see if he has a bit of time. And you are?"

"Oliver Bradford of Bradford-Stone from Leeds, England."

The woman's eyebrows raised. Instead of picking up her phone, she rose from her desk and walked to the office behind her. She tapped on the door and let herself in, the latch clicked behind her as she closed the door.

The bulletin board on the wall provided a diversion while Oliver waited. There were notices about volunteer opportunities and several upcoming community functions, including the Daughters of Lavinia Hawthorne-Covington Reunion celebration to be held on Patriots' Day weekend. It was either the day the people of Massachusetts celebrated their first win or the start of the Revolutionary War, Oliver wasn't clear on which. The date was mentioned on several of the flyers on the board including one about the Boston Marathon route.

The door opened, and the woman stepped out, followed by a man about Oliver's age. Oliver immediately recognized him from a video conference call they'd had in January.

Quinton Kayhill extended his hand. "Mr. Bradford, so nice to meet you in person."

"Oliver, please. Mr. Bradford is my uncle."

"Call me Quin. What brings you to Hawthorne?" Quin showed Oliver into his offices.

"Several things. Among which is a formal apology to you, and all involved in our company's ill-advised purchase."

"Unnecessary. The settlements that came with your written apologies were more than generous."

"Nevertheless, my uncle insists I apologize in person to everyone affected by my negligence."

Forced apologies were never fun. Oliver wasn't the only one to blame. There were just so many projects, and the Massachusetts one hadn't been very interesting, so he'd assigned it to his team and merely read the reports. At the time, he didn't realize that Uncle Pierceton expected Oliver to be involved in every new hotel project.

"Your negligence?"

"I didn't do my due diligence when I chose a firm to represent our interests and properties in Massachusetts. Even a simple internet search would have shown me that removing a block full of buildings, some of them historic, in the center of Hawthorne was not a wise decision." But he hadn't searched, hadn't vetted the estate agent or the law firm that a friend recommended, and hadn't visited the area.

Quin laughed. "It's not the worst mistake. I'm actually a little bit honored you even would've considered Hawthorne."

"I liked the name of your town," said Oliver "I have a list of people that I need to apologize to. Could you help me figure out the best way to do this?"

"Who's on your list?"

Oliver opened his note app and read the names from his list. "I've already met Dean Covington and his granddaughter Liberty."

Quin tilted his head. "You weren't driving a red convertible yesterday, were you?"

"Yes, I was the one who hit Liberty."

Quin shook his head and let out a low whistle. "Most everyone in town has already forgiven Bradford-Stone for the hotel incident, but we deliberately kept most of the details from Liberty. In case you haven't noticed, she has a grudge against people from England. However, yesterday's accident has most people siding with her. So you are back on the 'handle with caution' list."

"Understandable. I side with her too—over the accident. Considering the way we met, I would assume her grudge is more against me than my countrymen."

"Maybe. Though Liberty inherited quite a bit of her eighth great-grandmother's patriotism. My fiancée, Makenna, the owner of the antique shop, says that Liberty has never quite realized that the Americans won the Revolution and that we aren't still fighting."

"Exactly what do you mean?"

"Liberty is the only woman I know who refuses to watch any version of *Pride and Prejudice* because the actors are British and so is the author." Quin made his statement with a laugh.

Oliver rubbed his forehead. "In the few times I've been in the States, I've never met anyone with an aversion to me because of my nationality."

"That's because you never met Liberty—until now."

How would he ever gain her forgiveness, and would others hold him in contempt because of their friendship with her? The whole apology thing was supposed to have been the simple part of this business trip. Oliver absolutely had to get back into his uncle's good graces. "Well, one thing is for sure—she doesn't like me in the least."

Quin leaned forward in his seat. "My fiancée is not only Liberty's cousin, but she's also her best friend. If your goal is to have people not run you out of town, might I suggest you win over Makenna Wilson first? She can be your ally dealing with Liberty. I'll introduce you."

Oliver pondered the advice. "I hope you're right. My job depends on it."

# CHAPTER 5

The list of things to do before the reunion was impossibly long. Liberty scratched out "weed by goat shed." No one would notice if she did it anyway, and eventually, the goats would eat the weeds in their pen. They ate everything else. "Painting the bathrooms in the barn" could be done by the Monroe twins. Maybe they had some friends she could hire too. The chairs they used in the converted barn for meetings and weddings needed to be brought down from the loft to be dusted and cleaned. That job wouldn't take more than a couple of hours, and even one-handed, she could help with the cleaning.

By the time she reached the end of the list, she'd only eliminated a few of the items. Who could she get to drive all the errands she had? Mom hated freeway driving, and several of the errands would take Liberty to South Shore or Rhode Island. Grandpa didn't drive much anymore. Fiona, the cook, was busy and not exactly friendly, answering Liberty in monosyllabic grunts most of the time.

Tears filled Liberty's eyes. Impossible wasn't usually a word she used, yet it was the only word that came to mind. There wasn't enough money in the budget to hire a person to do all the things on the list that she couldn't do without the use of her shoulder. She'd completed all the low-impact things like phone calls and emails regarding orders and rentals of extra equipment.

Lisa tapped on her door before opening it. "Here is your lunch." She set a tray on Liberty's desk. "Are you crying? Are you in pain?"

"It isn't the pain. It is this list. I don't know how I can get everything done."

Lisa picked up the yellow legal pad. "I don't think everything on this list is strictly necessary."

"Such as?"

"Dusting the attic. Even if we do tours this year, a certain amount of dust is expected, especially among the younger girls—it'll make the attic all that much more mysterious. I didn't get the attic dusted for your first reunion. Did you mind?"

"I didn't notice."

"My point exactly. Also, I bet some of these places that you scheduled pickups will deliver for a small fee."

"What about the budget?"

Liberty's mother sat on the end of the bed. "Oliver gave us a decent-sized check to help cover hiring part-time help while you are incapacitated."

"When did he do that?"

"This morning."

"Did he check out?" Liberty couldn't keep the hopefulness out of her voice.

"How did you know he was here?"

"I needed a dust cloth for my shelves. He found me in the second-floor supply closet and asked for a towel."

"Oh, we were hoping you wouldn't realize he was here. It might be awkward."

"A warning would have been nice. I can't believe you let

him stay here." Liberty took a bite of her sandwich. Mayo, not salad dressing. "Did you make this?"

"No, Fiona did right before she left."

"She used yellow mustard, not Dijon. Did you tell her to use the Dijon?" For the last two weeks, Liberty had tried not to complain about the cook's bland food.

"Of course I did." Lisa took the other half of the sandwich and examined it. "I even got the jar out of the refrigerator myself. As for Mr. Bradford, we had open rooms and he couldn't find a close hotel last night. A paying guest is always welcome."

"Has he checked out yet?"

"No. He'll be here for a few days. If you can't be nice, avoid him."

"So I have to stay in my room and hide?"

"Considering Dean told you to rest and not work, I'd say yes." Lisa pulled a dusty book off of the shelf. "Haven't you wanted to read this book for forever?"

"But you need my help."

"I only had one room to clean this morning and three to refresh. Fiona had breakfast done, so I didn't need any help."

"I didn't think you cooked this morning. Your biscuits are better." Out of date refrigerator biscuits were better. Hopefully, Fiona would figure out the kitchen soon. Next time they hired a cook, Liberty would have applicants take a cooking test.

"That may be, but you know I can't keep up in the summer without help. Hiring a cook was one solution. Did you see the updates to the website? Fiona doing the cooking has given me the time I need to focus on marketing. Reservations for this summer are up already."

"I hate to see you work so hard."

"I'm only fifty, not dead and gone. And I enjoy doing web design. I'm not nearly as over the hill as you seem to believe. I still can turn around a room faster than most, and actually have it clean."

Her mother's point was well taken. For most of her early teen years, Liberty tried to race her mother in cleaning and preparing the rooms for the next guest. Rushing usually resulted in having to redo the work. Bathroom floors and precise corners on sheets needed to be done right, not just done.

"I wasn't suggesting you are over the hill. You were so tired this past winter."

"A bit of melancholy is all. I miss your dad, and this winter marked a halfway point for me. He's been gone now for as long as we were married before he passed. I was extra lonely this year."

"You hardly ever date. Why didn't you get remarried?"

"At one point, I thought of marrying just so you could have a father. Then I saw how much Covington House meant to you as you tried to learn to run it and dogging your grandparents' steps every bit of the way. Watching you with them, I realized I didn't need a man to be your father with Dean around. When your grandma died, you were in college and Dean needed me. And to be honest, even then I wasn't ready for another romance yet. I suppose if I ever met a man who made my heart race the way your father did, I might have seen where a relationship could lead. But I haven't met a man like that."

"You could still meet someone."

"If my heart raced like it did for your father, at my age, I might go into cardiac arrest."

"I thought you said you weren't that old."

"You underestimate what your father did to my heart. I understand you want to marry someone who is a friend, but I've never seen any of your friends get your heart racing. And just because someone doesn't start out as a friend doesn't mean they can't end up as one. Your father wasn't my best friend the day we married, but he was long before our first anniversary."

"Tell me about how you met."

"I've told you that story a million times."

"I want to hear it again."

"Well, it was a dark and stormy night. My friends and I were on our way back to Boston from a party. There had been a crash on the highway, and the police waved us into a detour. We didn't have GPS back then, and although a couple of my friends had cell phones, they weren't that common, and I didn't have one. I took a wrong turn someplace and ended up driving through Hawthorne. A large dog ran in front of the car, and I swerved and hit the brick wall, not too far from where you got hit yesterday. Your father came running out of the B&B. I think he was yelling. My head was bleeding, since my old beater of a car didn't have airbags, and he carried me inside. The second he stepped into the parlor, I knew he was the one. It took him longer to come to the same conclusion. A year later, we were married in the ballroom downstairs. It would have been sooner, but Covington men are stubborn."

"That's what Grandma said too."

"Now, about your list. Put the paper away, and we will tackle the list on Monday. You can't rest if you are worried about things you can't do today."

"But there is so much to do, it's impossible—"

Lisa put up her hand to stop her daughter. "This is Covington House. Impossible is not on the menu. Miracles happen here all the time."

Abigail's Antiques was not exactly what Oliver expected. Many of the pieces were old, even by his standards, while in one corner, the furniture looked new. When Quin opened the door, a bell rang and a woman with multiple pens in the hair piled on her head looked up. She came around the counter in a dress right out of a 1950s TV show.

Quin greeted her with a kiss. "This is Oliver Bradford of Bradford-Stone. And this is my fiancée, Makenna."

Makenna shook Oliver's hand. "Nice to meet you." She looked at Quin and raised an eyebrow.

Oliver cleared his throat. "I came to Hawthorne to apologize for the trouble we caused you over the winter. And instead, I believe I made things worse by running your cousin off the road."

"As far as the mess last winter, you have nothing to apologize for. The money you gave me more than compensated for the fire and other damage that was caused. But most of that was Wendell Smith's doing. And since he pled guilty to all charges, I don't have to worry about him for years."

"And your cousin?"

"That is between the two of you. From what I heard, hitting her was an unfortunate accident. I'm glad it didn't injure her more than a few bruises and a broken collarbone, and her helmet protected her from getting a concussion."

Awkward. Oliver looked around for something to talk about.

Makenna tilted her head. "I think I have something that you need." She hurried off to the backroom of the store.

"Does she do that often?" Oliver asked Quin.

"Not very, but when she does, you best purchase what she shows you. I can't exactly explain how she does it, but it is the one item in the world you need."

Makenna returned with an old silver inkwell and a penknife. "I'm not sure the items' origins; the set was acquired by Aunt Abigail years ago. I found it in the house the other day. I believe the inkwell and knife are the oldest items

I have in the shop at the moment, other than the wardrobe. Definitely pre-Revolution, maybe even late 1600s."

Before he could stop her, she put the items in his hand. Oliver expected the metal to be cold, but instead, it was warm, and he had a distinct feeling that something important needed to be written. He just had no idea what. "I don't even know what to do with them."

"You could set them on your desk or write something with them. There are online videos showing how to cut a quill and make ink."

He wasn't sure if the urge to purchase the odd items was from a need to have Makenna on his side or the type of impulse shopping that resulted in Uncle Pierceton cutting off his aunt's credit cards. "How much?"

Makenna named a price that seemed more than reasonable for the antiques, and Oliver completed the purchase.

Outside the shop, Oliver slid the bag into his coat pocket. "I'm not sure why I bought that. But don't worry, I won't return them."

Quin laughed. "Not if they were meant to be yours." He pointed to the statue. "They say she was a witch of sorts. The good kind. Odd things happen around some of her descendants. When I first met Makenna, I could have sworn there was a watch that stopped time. It's in the town museum now. I've visited the museum frequently and there is no time warp. Every once in a while, Makenna finds something that someone needs. If that inkwell and pen were meant to be yours, you'll know what to do with them. Are you hungry?"

"I could do with some lunch."

"Come to Sweet Memories Café with me. Some of their food is truly magical."

That was twice Quin mentioned magic. Obviously, the chamber of commerce director was all in when it came to promoting his town. Perhaps Quin held a bit too tightly to local folklore.

Lunch was better than average. The only truly amazing thing was the scones. They tasted exactly like the ones his mother's cook made when Oliver was little, even though they didn't look at all the same. When he complimented the baker, Keira, another cousin of Liberty's, she smiled as if she'd expected it would be the same recipe.

Oliver spent the rest of the afternoon going from business to business, chatting with those who were wronged or inadvertently harmed by Bradford-Stone's authorized agent. With one exception, everyone was very gracious. Quin's grandfather, an older man named Walter, barely nodded at the apology. It was as if he knew Oliver was being forced to be there.

Quin dismissed his grandfather's behavior. "Walter is very protective of Makenna. You should hear him after I return from a date with Makenna. The FBI and CIA could learn something from him about interrogation. We're engaged. Naturally, he's protective of Makenna's cousins too."

The B&B was quiet when Oliver returned. His room had been refreshed and there was no sign of the worn-out towel, but there was an extra one in the small bathroom. He sat at the desk and pulled out the penknife and inkwell, still unable to decide why he'd purchased them. He spent the next several hours surfing the internet, learning how to make quill pens.

# CHAPTER 6

Three days after the accident, the family parlor was full of laughter. Makenna came with three of Liberty's other cousins to cheer her up. Besides Makenna, Josie, Claire, and Keira were probably Liberty's favorite people in all the world.

Keira passed around a tray of her latest creations. "I'm not exactly sure, but I think these petit fours help you sleep better."

"I don't need to sleep better. I need the Brit out of the B&B." Liberty took a chocolate frosted one anyway.

Makenna chose a vanilla cake. "I met him two days ago. He is really nice, not to mention—*handsome*."

"Oliver's accent is so adorable. Reminds me of my favorite actor Benedict Cumberbatch," said Keira.

"When did you meet Oliver?" asked Liberty.

"Quin brought him into the café for lunch. Good thing Brant wasn't there to see me swoon a tiny bit. Oliver Bradford is as easy on the eyes as he is on the ears."

Josie dipped a carrot into the ranch dressing. "Agreed. Although he reminded me of Ioan Gruffudd when he was younger. Same eyes."

"Ditto." Makenna fanned herself.

Josie gave Makenna a playful shove. "Aren't you engaged?"

"Engaged is not dead," answered Keira. "We engaged women can still admire from a distance."

"He has Orlando Bloom's jawline," said Claire. "He came by my shop, looking for a journal yesterday."

Liberty shifted in her chair to find a position that didn't hurt as much. "Is this a game of *compare the man who hit me to hot British actors?*"

"No, only proving that not everything British is bad. Have you seen photos of the little royals? They are so adorable." Makenna searched on her phone and showed everyone the latest photos of Prince William's children. "You need to let this anti-Brit thing go, Lib."

"I've tried. It's part of me." She hadn't tried too hard; her pro-Revolutionary stand was one of those things that set her apart. It may have started as a joke, but she'd stayed with it too long to quit now.

"But look at what you're missing." Josie held up her phone and played a YouTube video that was a montage of various period drama actors set to "Sharp Dressed Man."

When the video was over, Claire shared her phone screen. "I like the 'It's Raining Men' version better. I wish cravats and twenty-piece suits were still in fashion."

"It isn't the suits—which aren't twenty pieces, by the way— it is the hats," said Makenna.

"No, it's the idea of marrying a rich man or an earl. It's the fantasy, the romance, and the costumes," said Keira.

The video, in combination with the song, was enough to make any woman's heart beat faster. Like hers had done in the supply closet. The smoldering look had to be a secret weapon of British men. Liberty held up her hand. "Fine, I concede England has some nicely built male actors in historic clothing."

"Wales, Scotland, and Ireland too. You so missed out not seeing Aiden Turner in *Poldark*." Makenna fanned herself dramatically.

Should Liberty warn Quin about his fiancée's British actor crushes? "I saw the shirtless memes, and I was tempted to see the PBS reruns. I watched the first one but didn't continue. How am I supposed to feel pity for someone who fought the Colonists?"

"There are always two sides to the story. One shouldn't blame the soldiers for the war."

The conversation continued in the same vein as the cousins tried to choose the hottest of the British actors. Liberty let the conversation go as the pain in her shoulder built. She checked her phone. She couldn't have another over-the-counter pain pill for an hour yet. She sneezed. The pain radiated through her shoulder. Her cousins stopped talking.

"I'll be honest, when Grandma Tansy told me you had a cold, I didn't believe her," said Keira.

"It's been better today, but I'm nearly out of lozenges." Liberty pulled one out of her pocket.

Makenna set down her phone. "Do you have a second bath bomb?"

"Kind of. They were smooshed to dust in the accident. I have half of the powder left." Liberty hadn't used the remedy yet as getting out of the bathtub had been difficult the first night, and she didn't want to have to call her mom again for help.

"We should get out of here and let you take a bath. Usually, it takes two of them to drive the cold completely away."

"I wish Grandma Tansy had something for healing bones. Six weeks in this sling will drive me batty. I start physical therapy next week. Hopefully that helps." However, no therapy could be magic.

Keira started packing up the treats she brought. "I've seen nothing for bone regeneration in her store, but didn't Lavinia heal Josiah's bones when he was injured?"

Makenna shook her head. "He was wounded by musket balls and had an infection. There aren't any stories I know about mending bones. But there are a lot of holes in the original histories—information we don't have yet about what Lavinia could do with her magic."

Liberty didn't doubt the existence of the magic anymore. Keira's baking and Makenna's ability to match objects that people needed to the right person were both far from normal occurrences. "So maybe I am sick and hurt so I can find the cure? Healing magic? Which I think Grandma Tansy might have. So I doubt my magic is the same thing."

"Your cold could have something to do with magic." Claire stacked the cups and plates on a tray.

"After rereading the histories, I think it could be the water from the old well. Is the well okay?" asked Makenna.

Liberty pointed to her sling. "Not up to prying the cap off the well yet."

"You don't need to pry the cover off," said Claire "There's a keyhole in the lid, like in utility hole covers."

"The cover is still heavy. And I don't have the key to the cover or the one to the padlock Grandpa put on," said Liberty.

"Then it won't be as easy as last time," said Keira.

Josie looked up from the container she was closing. "I didn't think it was easy last time."

"That's because you were only as tall as the well," said Keira.

"Ha. Ha. I am not that short." Josie needed heels to reach her claimed five-foot height. "You guys do not know how difficult it is to be vertically challenged. Last week, our director joked we could do *Annie* this season since I could

44

play the role, and they wouldn't need to have an understudy perform the matinees, since unlike a ten-year-old, I can act in back-to-back performances. I pointed out he'd still need to double cast the other children's roles. So we are doing *The Importance of Being Earnest*."

"I love that play." Makenna put an arm around Josie. "We like you just the way you are, high heels and all."

Keira and Claire gave Josie a ride home, leaving Makenna, who'd dawdled, taking the empty plates to the kitchen.

Makenna returned to the parlor and sat across from Liberty.

"What? I know you stayed for a reason."

"Do you really hate Brits?"

"I don't hate them. I'm not overly fond of the one in the hotel at the moment. But I don't hate him either."

"I know the avoiding-everything-English thing came out of your paper on Revolutionary war hero Deborah Sampson and getting to play Lavinia in the Hawthorne Independence Day parade for those years. Somewhere your obsession crossed the line. It isn't funny or quirky anymore."

"You mean the line where I can't vote on 'Who was the best Mr. Darcy?'"

"No. More like the racism line." Makenna winced as she said the word.

"Racist?" Liberty had never thought her all-things-American stance as anything other than American pride.

"Somewhere your 'Go, USA' took a turn for the extreme. I know everyone in town laughs, but..." Makenna shrugged.

"Wow. That is a wake-up call." Liberty thought about some of the comments she'd made through the years. "My aversion is a bit extreme. I've never wanted to hurt anyone, and I've never called them names."

"Maybe racist is too strong of a word. However, if you are missing out on the good things from another culture because of a battle two hundred and fifty years ago, I am not sure what else to call it."

Liberty wiped nonexistent crumbs from the coffee table as she pondered. "I have wanted to watch *Poldark*. The only reason I didn't was it was a BBC production. Which is a silly thing."

"I should warn you, the show takes place between the Revolution and the War of 1812, and it may make you see things differently."

"But I don't have to like the guy who hit me, do I?"

"I'm not forcing you to like anyone who hits you with a car—just hoping you'll be a bit more tolerant. I think most racist things start small and get taken too far. This has gone too far."

"Message received. I didn't think I was the R-word bad about this." Liberty pondered the uncomfortable feeling hitting someplace near her heart. Racist? How had that happened? She didn't want to be that person.

Makenna hugged Liberty before she left.

Liberty surfed through YouTube until she found the videos her cousins liked. They weren't too bad, and that one guy looked a bit like the Brit staying in the B&B. Maybe if she could learn to see the good in Mr. Bradford, she could put this thing behind her.

Oliver checked all the drawers in the room again to be sure he hadn't missed a personal belonging or a charging cord. There was little point in staying at the quaint B&B another day. He'd fulfilled his assignment to apologize personally to all those hurt by the hotel debacle. Still, he wasn't sure why Uncle Pierceton felt the need to have personal apologies. The Hawthorne Hotel wasn't the first deal to go south. At least everyone he met was gracious. Except for Walter.

Then there was Liberty. She wasn't on his list, but she needed an apology. He hadn't seen her since the morning she'd given him the ratty towel.

He'd thought of sending flowers to her but couldn't figure out if she was the type of woman who would like them or think he was trying too hard to make amends. Through Dean, Oliver had provided the funds available to hire part-time help for the work that Liberty could no longer do. It seemed everyone he spoke with had something to say about Liberty: she was a hard worker, great in the reenactments, and dedicated to Hawthorne.

It hadn't taken many conversations for him to realize the town wasn't opposed to a British company doing business. However the heir to the Covington House Bed & Breakfast carried strong feelings against the English and people humored her. And of course, no B&B owner ever wanted a new hotel going in down the street. There was a puzzle to unravel there. He'd stayed on an extra day hoping to speak to her, but she never came into the library or the parlor when he was around.

Bradford-Stone North America was sending a driver for the remainder of Oliver's stay. Oliver checked the email. He had enough time to have one last breakfast before relocating to another Boston area hotel.

An older couple sat at the dining room table. Oliver nodded at them before filling his plate at the sideboard. He poured himself a cup of coffee as, once again, there was no tea. The door to the kitchen opened and Liberty backed through, balancing a plate of scones. She set them on the table.

Oliver seized his last chance. "Good morning, Liberty."

"Mr. Bradford."

"Oliver."

"I understand you are leaving us this morning."

"And good riddance?" Oliver hoped she wouldn't agree.

For the barest moment, her face registered shock before smoothing into the calm mask of hospitality. "I hope you enjoyed your stay."

Oliver picked up a scone. "Are these yours?"

"No, I don't bake; I cook. Keira makes the best baked goods in town."

"I notice you don't have any tea."

A crease appeared between Liberty's brow as she turned to the sideboard. She opened a cupboard and searched through the containers. She pulled out an empty ceramic box. "How odd. We normally have a selection of herbal teas, many I make myself. And more traditional teas as well."

"You make herbal teas?"

"Yes. Did you know that three years before the Boston Tea Party, the society women of Boston signed a pact to boycott the tea imports?"

"No, I didn't." It was true, what Makenna had said about Liberty being a fountain of facts about the American Revolution.

"Many of the women experimented with herbal tea substitutes. A few of them are quite good. Of course, Covington House is most famous for our hawthorn berry tea."

"May I try some?"

"I'll be right back."

Oliver ate while he waited.

Liberty returned with an empty canning jar, her face pale. "My sincerest apologies. There was some sort of mix-up, and we are out."

Oliver stood and pulled out the chair next to him. "Please sit, you look…" There were no words that would not offend. Fortunately, Liberty took the seat without protesting.

"Surely, you can get more tea."

"I'm not sure how. These berries were special. They came from the tree in the front yard."

"The tree with the amazing pink blossoms?"

"That is the one."

"Then double my loss. That tree was what I was looking at when I forgot where I should be driving."

"Are you blaming the tree?"

"Absolutely not. Only lamenting that the tree was the source of two losses."

"Say 'British.'"

"Why?"

"I want to know if the meme is right?"

"You mean the one about hiding our 'T' since the Americans dumped the tea into the bay?"

Her cheeks colored—a better sight than the pale she'd been when she came back into the room.

"Bri-ish." Oliver accentuated the word as much as he could, earning him a smile.

"Do you really say it that way?"

"I may enunciate a soft 'T' in there normally. Since I was thinking about the meme, the 'T' disappeared altogether."

"Oh."

"I've heard several stories around town concerning you, and how you are the holdover from the Revolution."

"Maybe. I enjoy being in the reenactments. This year I'll miss the Patriots' Day one. Although with a sling I would have had to bow out, anyway. Since no one is planning on me being there, no harm."

"I am terribly sorry. I rarely go around running over beautiful women." The uncertainty in her look made Oliver want to backpedal his compliment, afraid he might have offended her more. "Or men, or anyone. I don't even occasionally. I mean, you are the first. And hopefully the last...

I'm bungling this, aren't I?" Apologizing to the building owners had been easier.

"Pretty much bungled. So I assume it's a sincere apology. False apologies are always too polished. My grandma said she could tell if I felt bad about stealing the cookie or getting caught based on how well worded my apology was."

"Interesting thought. I've always practiced mine so they sound right. Well, until the last few days. I wasn't going to stop in Hawthorne until I knew what to say to everyone about the hotel incident."

"Did you mean the apologies?"

"Yes." Of course he did. His job depended on him taking responsibility for his laziness.

"Not 'did you mean to give them.' Are you sorry?"

"I'm sorry people were hurt in the name of my company. After meeting them, I meant it even more. And I practiced them because that's what I've always done from the time my nanny made me apologize for dumping milk on my cousin's head." Maybe that is what Uncle Pierceton had wanted him to learn—that people, not numbers, were hurt. It wasn't about the money Bradford-Stone lost, it was about their good name.

"Obviously, you had no idea what kind of man Wendall A. Smith is. He was good at hiding that from most people. And the situation reflected poorly on you. His obsession with Makenna's money wasn't easy to figure out as even she didn't realize what the land was worth. So I get that. And I am sure your company wants you to mend bridges. However, if you were really sorry, you would have come a couple of months ago to apologize in person. A plane flight from Boston to London is shorter than from Boston to LA."

The words were as sharp as a bayonet. "Are you saying I'm not sincere?"

"When you told me you were sorry for hitting me, yes. But the way you talk about the other people you *had* to talk to makes me wonder if this isn't more of a duty than it should have been."

This woman was seeing a part of him he hadn't wanted to admit to himself. Oliver took a bite of his scone to avoid answering. A memory of sitting at the table with his mother filled his mind. In front of her was a plate of scones. She was lecturing him on something. He wasn't paying attention, but all he wanted was the scone. Oliver had the oddest feeling that if he'd paid more attention to his mother and less to his stomach, he might be a better man for it. "It's a person's duty to apologize when necessary."

Liberty rolled her eyes. "I'm afraid I was lecturing myself more than you. I owe you an apology that I don't want to give. It was wrong of me to give you that old towel. I also realized something rather uncomfortable about myself. The last few days, I judged you—and really your entire coun-try—based on the feelings of a sixth-grader who wrote an essay on the Revolutionary War, and I carried my anti-Brit thing too far. My dad died in the Middle East, and I think I connected my pain with the revolution... anyway, I'm sorry."

Unsure of what to do, Oliver covered her hand with his. An unexpected warmth filled him. There must be something more he could say.

His mobile vibrated, interrupting his thoughts. "Thank you. My driver is here. I need to go."

# CHAPTER 7

*C*lenching her jaw, Liberty finished the last repetition of the exercise. The best part of physical therapy was the flirty six-foot-two single therapist. Liberty didn't take him seriously as he flirted with every single female who came in, regardless of their age or marital status. However, focusing on him was better than the pain inflicted by what should be simple exercises.

"I told you the second visit would be easier." He grinned from ear to ear.

"Easier for who?"

"I don't feel any pain at all today." His wink wiped away a bit of the pain she had felt.

Forcing her eyes not to roll was almost as difficult as the last exercise. "Good to know."

"I understand you want to return to normal quickly, but pushing things harder will not get your bone to mend any faster." He pulled out the ice pack and wrapped it around her shoulder. "I'll be back in ten minutes."

The cold brought immediate relief to the area. Liberty leaned against the wall and closed her eyes. Why can't I heal faster? Why did Oliver have to drive on the wrong side of the road? Where was he now? Once again, the image of the Brit invaded her thoughts. She didn't toss him out. She wondered what he would say if he knew she'd enjoyed watching a BBC production the other night. The broken collarbone was helping her get caught up on all the television bingeing she'd missed out on the last several years. And she had to agree with her cousins about hot British actors. Although, she still couldn't decide which Mr. Darcy she liked best.

The timer pinged, and the therapist came over and removed the ice pack. Liberty picked up her exercise instructions at the front desk and went in search of her mother. Another problem with her injury was that she couldn't drive, requiring either Mom or Grandpa to take time away from the B&B or pay for a ride share.

Lisa pulled up to the curb, and Liberty climbed in the passenger door of her mother's car. The back seat overflowed with reusable shopping bags full of food. "I got all the shopping finished. I told you this would work."

"You don't need to go shopping three times a week, do you?"

"No, but it will work out. There are other errands to run."

"You always say things will work out."

"And they always do. Even in my darkest hour after Michael died and you were left without a father, it all worked out."

There was no use in arguing the point. Almost everything worked out. Although some things, like when her father died, left holes that never quite filled in. "Will you drop me off at Abigail's Antiques? I need to talk to Makenna. I can walk home."

"Sure. Will you go over to Red Leaves Books and check on the special order for Dean's birthday?" Lisa turned at the familiar 'Hawthorne three miles' sign.

"I'll also check with Keira about the cake."

"Thanks. See if Tansy thinks you need anything more for the cold. You still sound congested to me."

"I finished another box of tissues. I can't believe how fast they go."

Lisa laughed. "You probably used more in the last week than you did in your entire life, including when you used them to create tissue flowers."

"I didn't realize that tissue paper roses would turn out better with packing tissue paper."

Lisa pulled up to the curb in front of the antique store. "I'll see you in a while."

Makenna was helping customers, so Liberty ran the other errands first. Claire unboxed the out-of-print Ansel Adams photobook Lisa had ordered that morning.

"I love these black-and-white photos."

"He had amazing talent. Grandpa will love this."

"Would you like me to gift wrap the book?"

"Please. Then I don't have to hide the book going into the house. It's too big for my sling, anyway." Liberty sneezed.

"You still have that cold? It's been a week."

"Nearly the end, I think. Not sure how long they're supposed to last."

"Grandma Tansy keeps muttering about how you shouldn't have a cold at all. And proclaiming doom because of it." Claire used the signature store wrapping—paper decorated with red leaves.

"Doom?"

"Not really. She's being more dramatic than normal. She's checked on Keira's special baking several times this week."

"The memory scones are still working. We served them the other day for breakfast." Liberty's tasted like the strawberry frosting on her sixth birthday cake. That was the last time she'd chosen pink as a theme.

"All of Keira's special recipes are working. Even her newest ones. Which only sent Grandma Tansy muttering more." Keira had been the first of the cousins to discover any magical talents. Hers manifested in her baked goods from scones that brought back memories at a taste to cookies that would calm a combative board meeting. Each baked good had just a bit of magic to them.

"Why would Grandma Tansy think my cold had anything to do with Keira's magic?"

Claire shrugged. "Don't know. It isn't like Keira had made anything that cures people."

"Well, I would prefer to go back to my state of being in perfectly good health all the time. Between the cold and my shoulder, I'm dying here."

"Have you been coughing much?"

"No. I can only imagine how nasty that would be when a hard sneeze hurts my shoulder enough to make me cry."

Claire handed Liberty the wrapped book in a canvas tote marked with the Red Leaves logo. "The tote is on me. Consider it a get-well gift."

"Thanks. Carrying the book back would have gotten awkward."

Keira wasn't in the bakery. Liberty left a note with Aunt Ginger about the cake.

No customers lingered in Abigail's Antiques.

"Busy day?" Liberty asked.

"No more than usual. The shop is finally making a profit again without the flipped furniture. I'm going to hire a full-time employee so l can take a honeymoon and not worry about the shop."

"Walter will spy for you anyway and send you updates. Do you know where you are going?"

"Quin won't say. He told me to pack summer clothing."

"Not much of a hint since you are getting married at the end of July."

"I eliminated Antarctica." Makenna made a face. "How's the shoulder?"

"Slowly healing. I'm down to one ibuprofen before bed."

"Not bad for only one week. Five more to go."

"And the reunion is in three."

"How are the Monroe boys working out?"

"They are excellent workers. They got the flower beds cleared in record time." And had only pulled up a few flowers. Less than the goats would have.

"Let me know what I can do to help." Makenna flicked a speck of dust off the counter.

"Do you have any dried hawthorn berries? The ones from my trees?"

"I have some back at the house. What happened to yours?"

"The new cook threw out all the ones I ground for tea."

"She what?"

"She said they smelled bad."

"Don't you have other berries?" asked Makenna.

"Not enough. I gave you a bunch and sold the extra tea berries to my regular customers. The rest I used when I experimented making hawthorn berry jam."

Makenna made a face. "No offense, but that was a total failure."

"Agreed. But I still had twice the amount I needed for tea this year, even with the reunion."

"I can't believe she threw it all away without even asking you or your mom."

"It gets worse. She ordered hawthorn tea online. From China. No wonder the tea has been tasting odd for a while."

Makenna's brow furrowed. "When did the tea start tasting weird to you?"

"Not sure. Maybe mid-February? Mom gave me strict orders to leave Fiona to her, so I didn't go check then."

"Fiona? Isn't she Bethany's Aunt?"

"I didn't ask. Is that significant?"

"There are some things I want to check in a book I found." Makenna swiped at her phone. "Let me see if Walter can watch the store for an hour. I sent my new employee to do a furniture pickup."

Ten minutes later, Walter entered the front door. "Good thing I won our game, or I wouldn't have been so keen on leaving."

Makenna kissed the retiree on the cheek. "Thank you. Liberty and I should be back in an hour."

Oliver's fingernails dug into the vinyl seat as Zetta whipped through the streets of Boston with the agility of a racecar driver. For the past two days, his new assistant had shuttled him from one property to another in his search of a hotel location. He couldn't relax when she drove, which was an enormous problem as he needed to look at the area surrounding each property. Instead, he was looking at the road ahead, hoping that she wouldn't hit an intersection on a yellow light, a sure sign that she would accelerate.

The light turned red. Zetta slammed on the brakes. "Yes, pole position!"

Oliver looked up the term yesterday to discover it was a racing term for the person who qualified with the best time and had the best starting position for the race. This led him down a rabbit hole of videos of NASCAR races and a growing surety that Zetta missed her calling in life when she chose hospitality management as a college major.

The light changed to green, and Oliver gripped the armrest on the door.

"I will not crash. And if I did, holding onto the door won't help you."

"Sorry." Oliver forced his grip to relax.

"You need to loosen up. Come out with me tonight." Her invitation repeated ones given the previous two nights.

"I still don't think that is wise." Convincing her that her job was only to drive him around was more difficult than getting her to slow down. The standard non-fraternization lines didn't seem to faze her.

She stopped at the next light and turned to him. "I know where a great band is playing."

"Thank you, no." Oliver wasn't sure how to end her constant invitations without alienating her.

The light turned, and they drove the rest of the way in silence.

Zetta found a parking space and turned off the car.

"I would like to take public transportation back to our hotel so I can get a feel for what the tourists might see. You don't need to wait."

"You're sure?"

"Yes."

She frowned. "See you later then."

The real estate agent was competent and had all of his facts and figures. Still, Oliver could not imagine a Bradford-Stone hotel on any of the properties he'd seen. The old factory site he was viewing needed to have asbestos mediation, and who knew what other environmental concerns lurked below the surface—a potential nightmare that had kept interested buyers at bay for years. Once that would be cleared, the location wouldn't be that bad. Convenient to what the locals called a 'T' station for the trolley and subway, it would be easy for tourists to navigate the area. He walked the perimeter of the property again as the agent watched.

Oliver returned to the agent's car. "Thank you for showing these to me. What's on the schedule for tomorrow?"

"I emailed you some other properties of interest. None of them have T access, but a few are on the train lines."

They shook hands and parted ways.

Oliver checked the map on his mobile before walking the two blocks to the nearest T station. Tiny green leaves adorned trees planted on either side of the street. The walkways were free from rubbish. All in all, it was one of the better walks to public transit from any sites he'd looked at so far. The green line trolly was as clean as could be expected and made a stop at the science museum before crossing over the river to Boston. The area wasn't as upscale as Back Bay where his current hotel was located, but he could play off of the eclectic charm in the area. Not everyone needed—or even wanted—to be surrounded by high-end shops. Of course, it didn't have the personality the B&B had, either. To the staff at the large hotel, Oliver was just another tourist. At least they hadn't connected him with one of their competitors.

The trolley continued to fill with each stop. Thinking on a crowded train never worked. Oliver got off early and walked the last several blocks to his hotel under cloudy skies. Everything about the hotel was bland, no different from dozens of other rooms he'd stayed in—both in Bradford-Stone and other chains. It was missing the uniqueness of the B&B, as well as the friendliness, and the not so friendliness. Oliver chuckled out loud. What he was missing was a verbal sparring match with Liberty.

"Here is a passage about washing blisters in water from the well," said Makenna. "I wish I could remember where I read about tea made from the well water."

"So the water has some magic?" Liberty opened another dusty book, not sure what she was looking for.

"It makes sense. The entire story about Lavinia saving Josiah centers on the water. We broke into the well thirteen years ago because we thought there was something magic in the water."

"If I've lived around magic my entire life, how come I have no power or control over the water?"

"I don't have any control. I do what the magic wants me to do. Like I'm a conveyer. Maybe you are meant to protect the water like a guardian." Makenna closed her book. "Think. Why did we decide we needed to use hawthorn berries to make tea that night? Did your grandmother serve hawthorn berry tea?"

"Not regularly. If she had, we wouldn't have gone to the trouble to pick those old dried-up ones."

Makenna pulled up her sleeve to her elbow. "I still have the scar from the scrape I got climbing Lavinia's tree. Grandma Tansy refused to sell me any of her scar cream."

"I didn't scar."

"Of course you didn't. You drank the well water your entire life. You had super immunity. When you hired the cook, you started staying out of the main kitchen and didn't get as much well water. I think that, in combination with the change in the tea, did something to your immunity. Hence the cold. Oh, that reminds me…" Makenna opened her genealogy app. "Fiona is Bethany's aunt on her mother's side."

"I didn't think you could look up things on living people."

"I can if they had me help them and put their information in. Bethany's mother was trying to prove her application for membership in Daughters of The American Revolution for her and her sisters. She insists the qualifying ancestor lived in Hawthorne. I'm having some problems with it as I can't find a birth record for Bethany's seventh great-grandfather or intentions of marriage for his mother. It isn't terribly uncommon that she married a man with the same last name, but the son was born during the Revolutionary War. There may be another line…"

"And this applies to our water discussion how?" asked Liberty.

"It's not. You mentioned your cook and… Anyway, I am sure the water has healing properties."

"Do you think Grandma Tansy knows this? Why wouldn't she tell me? I could have gotten rid of my cold quicker."

Makenna laughed. "As odd as she's been lately, you're lucky she gave you her cold cure. She has been closing the shop at strange hours for the past few weeks. Claire and I have searched every social media site there is hoping to find Eden. Since she is Tansy's only real granddaughter, Eden needs to know."

"Nothing?"

"Not even a whisper. I've thought of asking Carter if he knows where she is, but I don't want to go there. After all, it is only a guess that their breakup had anything to do with her not returning to Hawthorne in a decade."

"It hasn't been that long."

"Close."

"Maybe she'll come to the reunion. Even though she didn't get an invitation, she should know when it is."

Makenna stood and dusted off her skirt. "Maybe there is something I missed in the room behind the clock. Will you get the flashlight from the kitchen drawer?"

Liberty grabbed the huge flashlight and watched Makenna stop the pendulum of the grandfather clock and open up the back panel. The space seemed smaller than it had when they were younger. "I can't believe that things just appear in here."

"I don't know if they *appear*. Quin and I found a trap door that goes into the cellar. I've wondered if Grandma

Tansy is paying someone to sneak in here and leave things. I don't think she could climb up here herself."

"Isn't your cellar locked?"

"Locks only keep honest people out." Makenna took the flashlight from Liberty and slowly scanned the shelves. She stopped. "Where did this come from?" Makenna reached back on one of the top shelves out of Liberty's view. She pulled out a round box barely larger than her hand.

"What is it?"

Makenna took back the flashlight. It wasn't a round box exactly, but more like a small wood drum. The top and the bottom were wood disks, the sides were short wood strips held in place by metal bands. On one side there was a small round hole in the wood. "I think it's a canteen. Coopers used to make them like mini water barrels."

"How old?"

"I can't tell in this light. Possibly as old as the Revolution or even the French and Indian War."

"And this wasn't here last time you checked?"

Makenna handed Liberty the canteen. "No. Let me check for anything else." She peered into the shelf again. "There are some papers." Makenna retrieved those too. "Let's get to where there is better light."

They returned to the parlor, leaving the clock open.

Liberty inspected the spaces between the wood slats of the canteen. "It doesn't look like it would hold water."

"Soldiers had to keep the canteen moist to keep the wood sides tight. The container would be painted too. I've only seen them in museums."

Liberty hit the side of her head with her palm. "I should have recognized this from my reenactment things. But an old canteen doesn't help us much."

Makenna turned over the canteen, inspecting every inch. "It is interesting that we were discussing water, and a canteen shows up. And one that is museum quality too. Maybe the letters will help. Judging by the paper, they are about the same age."

10 May 1775

Dearest Willoughby—

My father says I am not to write to you anymore after your disgrace in the Colonies. We only heard the news last week.

How could you have gotten your entire company lost in the fog? Is it true—will there be a court-martial? That you are no longer a captain?

Father wishes me to cancel our engagement. I do not wish to. Even if you are stripped of your rank, I will be faithful. I know I am being terribly scandalous, but I'd rather proclaim my love for you and have my father know all than marry someone I loathe. I wish we could have wed before you left or that we had shared more than a few kisses. Do not think less of me for such thoughts. Mary's husband died in battle, but she has their son. If you are to die, what will I have of you but a memory, a kiss in the garden, and a lock of your hair?

It is not enough. You must return to me.

Yours faithfully,

Katherine

"Willoughby? As in Willoughby Pitt, the Captain that Lavinia overheard?" Liberty never thought to hear the name outside of the tale of that night. "He was demoted and injured at Bunker Hill and returned to England a few months later."

"I don't know. I wonder if I can find him in my genealogical database. A young unmarried captain must have been from a family that purchased him a commission in the army." Makenna opened the next letter.

22 July 1775

Dearest Willoughby—

Your sister tells me you have been wounded in battle at a place called Bunker Hill. I hope you still live. It is awful that I hope your commanders decide you must return home. Father has picked four men for me to choose a suitor from. I hope to prolong the process long enough for you to return to me, for then we can run to Gretna Green.

I will not tell you the names of the men my father has chosen as they are all known to you by either title or rank. None of them are so brave as to fight for the Crown and put down the rebellion like you. Oh, that I was brave enough to run away, to follow my letter into your arms.

I pray for you each night.

Your most faithful,

Kathrine

"This is the last one." Makenna carefully unfolded the paper holding it by the edges as she had the other two. The ink on the last was smeared making it hard to read.

*2 September 1775*

*Dear —*

*I am not even sure how to address this, Mister seems so cold, but I know not your rank.*

*By the time you receive this, I will be wed. The first banns are to be announced Sunday. Father and Mother are pleased with the match. It is not proper for me to address you as I wish.*

*I have cried buckets of tears, but no one will listen to me. I don't care that we might be subject to poverty when you return. Know that I do this unwillingly. I have no choice. There is no escape for me.*

*I pray that you live through this terrible disturbance in the Colonies. I cannot hope that you find another to love, though I do not wish you the sadness I currently feel and am doomed to live with the rest of my days.*

*Farewell, my love,*

*Katherine*

"How sad. I feel bad for him." Makenna folded the letters.
"I do too. I never thought I would."
"I think then, like now, war hurt many on both sides of the battle. He lost his rank and his love because of the fog."

"I don't feel bad for his rank, but to lose Katherine is sad. Although it's still better than if the British had won the battle at Concord too."

Makenna picked up the canteen again. "So how was this supposed to help us?"

"I have no clue. Unless the story is a lesson for me about the British and not judging."

"I'd better get back to the store. I'll research Willoughby and see if I can figure out why these were in the closet. I'm still not used to things appearing in here."

Liberty walked back to the B&B feeling sorry for the poor captain. Lavinia may have saved lives with her dense fog, but there were still casualties.

# CHAPTER 8

Rain ran down the windows of Covington House, a fitting way for April to start. No matter how she counted the days, Liberty was only two weeks into her six-week recovery. Nothing would speed up the healing. At the sound of footsteps, Liberty turned from the window.

Grandma Tansy entered the family's private parlor. "There you are. How is your cold today?"

"Finally gone, I think."

"Keira told me that Makenna said your new cook threw out all of your dried hawthorn berries for tea."

"She said they smelled weird. But I noticed nothing wrong with them last time I set out some for the breakfast buffet. I dried them the same way Grandma taught me." One of Liberty's earliest memories was washing the berries in the big tub on the screen porch. Then spreading the red hawthorn berries on trays to be stacked around the wood-burning stove out in the old summer kitchen where they sat for three days drying. The year Liberty turned seven, the wood stove was replaced by an electric dehydrator Grandpa built. The process still took three days but was more environmentally friendly.

"Your grandma had you helping her from the time you could walk. I'm not doubting that you prepared them correctly. Your cook's nose doesn't know what is good when she smells it. When exactly did she throw them out?"

"Fiona didn't say. I hired her around Valentine's Day. Mom had me stay out of the kitchen while she trained her, so sometime near the end of the month."

"What a waste. Do you need more berries?"

"I froze some to use in our all-berry ice cream in the summer, but not enough to restock my supply for tea. Makenna had some but only enough for a few weeks' worth."

"Well, you're in luck. The tree behind my shop had a bumper crop this year. Usually I leave a bunch for the birds, but this year I picked them all. I stuck gallons of them in Ginger's walk-in freezer. I think she thought I was crazy."

"How many gallons?"

"Don't know, maybe forty. Enough that Ginger has been muttering about getting rid of them."

Forty gallons would replace all Liberty had lost. She'd had complaints from some of her regular visitors about the new tea recipe. "May I buy them from you?"

"No."

Liberty's hopes fell.

"I'm giving them to you. Make sure you drink only your own tea, and don't let that cook make it for you."

"Great, I'll drive—" Nope, Liberty wasn't driving anywhere. "I mean, I'll ask—"

"Nonsense, I asked Ginger to have someone drop them off later today and to deliver them only to you."

"Thank you so much."

"I knew I saved them for a reason. The tree always knows when we are going to need more berries. My mother told me that back around 1917 all the trees here and behind my store produced so many berries that the Covington women didn't know what to do with them all. My grandmother told everyone to dry all that they could. That is why they were all prepared when the Spanish flu came to town. Not one resident of town who used my grandmother's flu elixir died from the flu. Of course, there were several who refused to use the remedy. Like today, there will always be people who doubt the wisdom of the Covington women."

"Don't worry, I'm going to keep these berries under lock and key, if I must. I already moved the frozen ones into the family freezer. I even gave up my stash of chocolate ice cream space for them."

"Goes to prove you are a Covington woman. You chose the berries over the ice cream. Did your Grandpa ever tell you about the trees?"

"A little. The old one by the road was planted back in 1758 on the day Lavinia was born. All the other hawthorn trees here, along with the one behind your shop, are from shoots or seedlings from the original tree. Every time a female Covington is born in the house, a new tree has been planted. However, only a few of them are still alive today."

"And where is your tree?"

"On the south side of the little stock pond."

"Did it produce much last year?"

Liberty shook her head. "Lots of blooms but very little fruit."

"Hmm. And this year?"

"I haven't checked." Other than Lavinia's tree, none of the other trees were in full bloom. The first day of April was still early spring for this part of Massachusetts.

"You should. Plants are living things too. They like to be admired. You need to go tell her how beautiful her buds are." Grandma Tansy's advice was no stranger than normal for her.

Liberty mulled over the idea. It couldn't hurt. There were enough Covington stories about the hawthorn trees and the berries to risk looking silly talking to a tree. Keira used hawthorn berries in some of her magical creations. "I'll go visit the tree as soon as it stops raining."

"Rain isn't hurting the tree, and it won't hurt you. Besides, moving around is better than sitting inside feeling sorry for yourself."

The urge to deny the accusation welled up inside, but Grandma Tansy's narrowed eyes kept Liberty from saying the lie out loud.

"I know it's hard for you not to do everything around here. But sometimes people need to slow down and let the unimportant things slide. Now, walk me to the door since you are going outside, anyway. I'd stay for a cup of tea, but as we concluded, the hawthorn berry tea here is no good."

No car waited for Grandma Tansy.

"Did you walk here?"

"No, one of my customers dropped me off. Someone will be by in a moment who can give me a ride. They always do."

Grandma Tansy toddled off under a red polka-dot umbrella. No sooner did she step foot on the sidewalk in front of Covington House than a car pulled over, marked with the delivery phone number for the pizza place less than a half block from Grandma Tansy's shop. Liberty laughed. If it had been her, no one would have stopped, and she would have been drenched because the pizza driver would have splashed a puddle all over.

Liberty turned and walked down the graveled path to the stock pond. Not that the few goats and chickens needed a pond. There hadn't been a cow on Covington land for years. Last year, Liberty looked into the requirements to keep one as part of a petting zoo, as the zoning waiver the B&B had for the goats allowed her to have a cow and a horse as part of the educational experience of the historic house and farm. It didn't take her long to realize that, although she had the land, she didn't want to add the cost or daily tending of either animal to her list of chores.

As she neared her tree, the rain slowed and the clouds lifted. Late afternoon sun glinted on the leaves and the remaining pink buds. Liberty traced the initials her father had carved into the tree on her tenth birthday. Another tradition dating back over 250 years, it was a way to know which tree belonged to whom. The last person to have a tree planted on the property before Liberty was her great-aunt Abigail, Makenna's grandmother. Her tree was near the barn.

"Hello, Treebie. I thought I was so smart when I named you that. My apologies." Liberty walked around the tree counterclockwise, running her left hand along the trunk. "I see a bird is building a nest up there."

Liberty squinted to study the nest and was rewarded with a raindrop falling on her nose. "Do you get lonely back here? I hope not. It is one of the prettiest places on the property. Mostly because I don't encourage visitors to come back here. Everyone sees Lavinia's tree. I hope you don't feel left out." Liberty felt marginally silly for talking to the tree the way she had when she was little. She hadn't talked to the tree for a couple of years. As mixed up as her life had been lately, it couldn't hurt.

"Things aren't going so well. I got hit by a car. Oh, and the new cook threw out my hawthorn berries. But Grandma Tansy saved the day with forty gallons of frozen berries." As Liberty unloaded her worries on the tree, they didn't seem so bad. The rain stopped, and the sun came out from behind a cloud, turning the flowers of the tree into glittering masterpieces.

After verifying the last slide uploaded, Oliver turned off his computer and removed his headphones. Everything was ready for tomorrow's early morning call with his uncle to present the top three properties he'd found. Oliver stretched and pulled out the room service menu. Staying in his room was the only way to avoid Zetta. Her daily invitations for them to see each other outside of work hours had increased from daily to practically hourly. The convenience of having rooms next to each other quickly became anything but. As usual, her television blared loud enough to be heard through the wall separating the non-adjoining rooms he'd requested to overrule arrangements at check in. He didn't want to send any mixed messages. The relationship was only business.

Over the last several days, he'd learned if he left his room, she would find him in a matter of minutes. He'd wondered if she had some sort of mini cam watching the hall as she binge-watched action movies. Oliver wished for the return of the Victorian Era men's club like his great-grandfather had belonged to. Then he would have a place to escape into where she couldn't follow. Even the hotel's sauna wasn't completely safe, as Zetta was not above waiting outside of the men's locker room for him. At least so far, she hadn't followed him in.

Oliver was trapped—as sure as if he were chained in the Tower of London in the time of the Tudor kings.

He picked up the faux leather-covered menu and flipped through the familiar offerings. Of course, the room service menu hadn't changed since lunch. It was still early for dinner, anyway. He looked around the generic room. Why did hotels build this way? Impersonal. The seascape water-color above his king-size bed could have been of almost any beach in the world. The serviceable carpet was probably the same color as every other hotel room in the chain. If he changed the tint to add a touch of green, the room could be in any Bradford-Stone hotel where only the elite suites were personalized.

Oliver paced around the room. He had to get out or go mad.

Funny, at Covington House he'd never felt confined in his room. Probably because he never ran out of things to look at and explore, like the collection of books by Massachusetts authors. There were only ten books, but that was more than enough for the average stay. The paintings were accompanied by brief histories. The antique and replica furniture were unique and fascinating. The comfortable chair in the corner and the lace doily under the lamp all invited one to enjoy the space.

Oliver opened the MTBA schedule on his phone. The next train for Hawthorne left South Station in twenty-five minutes. Perhaps he could escape his prison. Zetta wouldn't expect him to take a train this late in the afternoon.

Switching his work shirt for a gray t-shirt, and his loafers for a set of trainers, Oliver dumped out the duffle he normally took down to the large hotel gym and loaded it with his laptop, a change of clothes, and his shave kit. With any luck, Zetta would think he was going to work out again and not look for him for five minutes. He tossed the Red Sox sweatshirt he'd picked up as a souvenir over his shoulder. Although the rain had stopped, it wasn't warm enough to go out without a jacket.

The elevator door closed. Zetta hadn't caught him yet. He hurried through the lobby and across the street to the T-station. According to the readout on the wall, the next T wasn't for five minutes. Oliver hurried out the exit on the other side of the T-station and hailed one of the many yellow cabs that waited for passengers too tired to walk to their final destination.

At South Station he found the correct commuter rail and boarded. Still safe.

The ride out to Hawthorne took long enough that he finished three chapters in the ebook he'd downloaded before he left Leeds. Oliver texted Dean to see if there was a room for the night. Dean didn't answer.

However he received several texts from Zetta.

—*Where are you?*

—*I don't see you in the gym?*

—*Are you ok?*

—*Oliver?*

Gone out for the evening.

That was more than she needed to know.

—*Where?*

Don't worry, I'm not driving. You have the night off.

The texts ended. Oliver wondered if Zetta was wandering around Back Bay looking in restaurant windows. The best April Fool's Day joke he never planned.

The conductor announced Hawthorne station as the next stop. Still no answer from Dean. Oliver hoped they weren't full on a Thursday. He double-checked the MBTA app. If the B&B was full, he had two trains back into the city tonight he could catch.

The station was a mile from the B&B. Oliver pulled on his sweatshirt and turned down the street, his map app showing the shortest route. It was also the route with the most puddles on the uneven sidewalk. Water soaked through his trainers and into his socks. He should have packed two extra pairs.

As the B&B came into sight, raindrops began to fall. Oliver quickened his pace, and so did the rain. Water ran down his neck, so Oliver pulled up the hood of his sweatshirt and commenced jogging. The first puddle, he dodged. The second, he didn't, splashing water up to his knee. If it were possible that some force had wrung the clouds of all their water at once, every drop of it landed on Oliver.

On the porch, he shook himself off as much as possible and pushed back the hood of his sweatshirt before opening the front door.

Liberty stood behind the check-in desk. "What are you doing here?"

# CHAPTER 9

*I*f the person who came in the door had been wearing a spacesuit, Liberty could not be more surprised. Oliver stood, dressed in a Sox hoodie, dripping all over the entry floor. Her racing heart was because of the shock, nothing more. "I mean, Mr. Bradford—Oliver—sorry, I wasn't expecting you." She grabbed a towel from the shelf behind the check-in desk and held it out to him.

He laughed and took the towel. "I texted Dean asking if he had a room for the night."

"Grandpa is at the community center. Bingo night. He probably hasn't even read your message. Nothing gets between him and his cards."

Oliver removed his hoodie. The t-shirt underneath clung to the sweatshirt for a moment, riding up high enough to expose a well-defined set of abs. Liberty squelched the sudden urge to fan herself and turned her attention to the laptop. Several rooms were empty, including the one he stayed in before.

"There are a couple of rooms—" Liberty looked up from the screen. Oliver's biceps flexed as he ran the towel over his hair. Did all British men hide bodies like this under their proper jackets? The list of actors Makenna gave her ran through her mind. The period drama montage videos replayed in her mind. Sweet iced hawthorn berry tea. Liberty could use a cool glass right now.

He lowered the towel and caught her staring. He grinned. "Do you have a room?"

Liberty moved her eyes back to the screen. "Yes." Her voice squeezed. "You can either have the room you stayed in last time or room six, the Josiah room, is available."

"Josiah?"

"Named for my eighth great-grandfather who fought in the Revolution." Liberty gathered strength from the thought. Her grandfather helped send the Brits home. Like she should do with this one. He may be handsome and have abs to make a Greek sculpture cry, but he was a visitor. One rule of the hospitality industry was never to get involved with guests. And for the first time in her life, Liberty was tempted to break the rule, knowing it would only leave her with a heartache that hurt worse than her shoulder.

"Is the room available the entire weekend?"

"Not just the night?" Her voice squeaked again. Too bad her cold was gone. She couldn't blame her wavering voice on a physical ailment.

"I'm not sure. After an early morning call to Leeds, I don't have any more work this weekend. It would be nice to stay here."

Liberty glanced at his bag. He traveled light. "Where is your driver?"

"She has the weekend off too."

She? Liberty had pictured his driver as a male. Maybe the driver was old and blind. Spending all day in a car with Oliver would put Liberty's hormones into overdrive. "Both rooms are available through Monday." With only three of the twelve rooms occupied this weekend, almost everything was available.

Oliver pulled out his wallet and handed over a credit card. "Book me to leave Monday morning."

Liberty tapped the information into the computer. She ran Oliver's card and handed him the key.

He held up the key chain. "There is something comforting about a key over the plastic reader cards."

"Those systems cost a fortune for a small place like this. It's easier to rekey the lock if a key goes missing."

"Aren't you worried about people making duplicates?"

"Not really."

"Your security isn't—" He paused.

"It isn't—as in nonexistent? We have a couple of cameras on the front door and parking lot, but pretty much we trust our guests. Every once in a while, a book or something will go missing, but ninety percent of the items end up being returned with a note of apology and, often, money or other compensation."

Oliver's mouth hung open for a second. "Towels? Knick-knacks? They all get returned?"

"Usually. There are only a few items that disappeared over the years that haven't come back. Mostly towels. There are only three or four thefts of those a year."

"The good towels or the other ones?"

Liberty's cheeks warmed at the reference to the ratty towel she'd given him. "The good ones. We don't normally give the guests the retired ones."

"So I was a special case?" The golden flecks in his brown eyes sparkled.

"I already apologized."

"Sorry, that was a poor jest on my part. Speaking of which, I should go upstairs and change. I'm afraid I've made a mess of the floor."

She shrugged her good shoulder. "Only water. Do you need extra towels? I have the good ones."

"Two?"

Liberty handed him the towels. Oliver took the stairway next to the desk. Liberty tried not to admire the view of the back of his jeans. If he were local, she'd be tempted to get to know him better. Forget that—she was already tempted. They would have a date. Tonight. She'd never had a summer romance or a vacation fling. So maybe she could, just this once. She pushed the insane thought away. It was one thing to not dislike Brits. It was another to want to date one.

The Josiah room resembled a nineteenth-century version of a man cave. The furniture was thicker and the colors deeper than the other room Oliver had stayed in. A carved and painted replica of a Colonial Era firearm hung above a converted gas log fireplace. A small notice under the carving stated the gun was a replica and for display only. The painting in this room depicted a haze covered eighteenth century battlefield. Through the cannon smoke, the redcoats retreated. The small bathroom contained all modern amenities.

His stomach rumbled. Oliver quickly changed out of his wet clothing, even as rain continued to run down the window. Takeaway would be on the menu tonight. Oliver left his trainers next to the radiator and ran down to the lobby in stocking feet.

No one was at the B&B's front desk, and the puddle where he stood earlier had dried. Liberty came through the employee-only door. "Did you need something?"

"Do you have a list of restaurants that deliver other than the Chinese restaurant? I had Asian last night. Or is there a service?"

"Mom made her Boston baked beans and sourdough bread

for dinner. I was just going to eat. Do you want to join me?"

"Don't you need to watch the desk?"

"We don't have any more guests expected tonight. I can watch the door from the kitchen." Liberty kicked a door wedge under the employees' only door to prop it open.

"You sure there is enough?" Not that he was opposed to eating with Liberty. All the perks of a date with none of the awkwardness.

"Mom usually makes enough for a crowd. Even with what she took to some shut-in neighbors and this couple that recently had a baby, there is still two- or three-days' worth of food for the three of us." She beckoned him to follow her.

"I didn't think you served guests meals other than breakfast."

"We don't."

Oliver paused.

Liberty turned on a light in the large kitchen. The room was out of place in the eighteenth-century building. Except for an old sink in the corner, everything was stainless steel and functional. Yet it was perfectly functional for a kitchen that needed to be inspected by the health department.

"Come on. I am not trying to poison you. Promise."

"I wasn't worried about that. I didn't think that you really wanted to eat with me."

"I thought we agreed to be friends. Friends don't let friends starve."

So much for the date part of the evening.

Even with the sling, Liberty was deliberate and efficient in her movements. She took two bowls from the cupboard. "Would you mind slicing the bread? I do an uneven job with my left hand." She used her chin to point to a crusty loaf of bread sitting on a cooling rack.

"How is your shoulder?"

"Improving. Physical therapy is helping. I wish my shoulder would heal faster."

"Have you been able to hire the help you need?"

Liberty ladled beans into the bowls. "Enough. I've let a few things go from my list."

"I could help you this weekend. I know my way around hotels."

"How are you at painting barns?"

Oliver cut four slices of bread and put them on a plate. "I've never painted a barn before, but I painted the bathroom in my flat. So I know the basic drill."

"I'll find you a paintbrush."

"Something as big as a barn, wouldn't you use a paint sprayer?"

"We aren't painting the big barn. I hired that out. We are painting the goat shed and the chicken coop. The little things that they wanted to overcharge to do."

Oliver carried the bread to the corner table.

"Butter is in the crock on the counter." Liberty balanced a bowl in each hand as she crossed the room.

The scent of warm bread hung in the air. As she approached, other aromas surrounded him. "Smells good."

"Have you ever had Boston baked beans before?"

"Not homemade."

Liberty grabbed two glasses and went to an old sink tucked near a door. She turned the 50s-style faucet, but no water came out. "That's odd." She stuck her head under the sink. "Someone turned the shut-off valve. Will you turn the faucet on, please?"

Her cheeks pinked as if asking him to do something she probably could have done herself embarrassed her. The blush was endearing. A primal part of Oliver longed to see her blush again.

On his hands and knees, Oliver reached under the sink and turned the knob. Above him, he heard water rushing into the sink. Liberty let out a cry of dismay.

Oliver stood and stared at the rust-colored water. The scent of rotten eggs rose like steam.

"What is wrong with my water?"

"Is this municipal water?" asked Oliver.

"No, it's our well. The water is…" Tears formed in Liberty's eyes.

The smell was almost enough to cause him to tear up as well. Oliver turned off the tap.

Liberty turned from the sink and discreetly swiped at her eyes. She opened a huge double-door refrigerator. "I have some soft drinks. Would you like one?"

Anything other than the water. "Yes, please. I'll even take grape soda."

"I don't have any grape. There is root beer, cream soda, and lemon-lime…"

"Lemon-lime." Oliver reached over her shoulder and took a can. Liberty chose the cream soda.

At the table, she stirred her beans, her attention on the sink beyond him.

The baked beans were much better than he expected them to be. "This is good."

"It's mom's secret ingredient. Makes them the best beans around."

"What is that?"

"If I told you the secret ingredient, it wouldn't be secret anymore." Liberty's eyes sparkled when she laughed.

Oliver buttered a section of his bread. "This is good too."

"Mom used to do all the cooking for the B&B, but she is slowing down a bit. I didn't think she could handle the summer crowd this year. That is why we hired a morning cook. I miss mom's cooking though. And considering how much cooking she is doing at night, I think she misses being in the kitchen too."

"Do you cook?"

"Not as well as Mom, but I can get a decent meal served when I have two hands."

"Are you rubbing that in?"

She adjusted the sling. "Sorry, no. I'm frustrated. I don't like being slowed down. Not when there is so much to do. And I have a hard time having others do things I could do myself."

"Is that why the officer called you Miss Independence?"

"You caught that?" The rhetorical question didn't need an answer. "I'd rather do things myself than have other people do them—" She paused. "—differently."

Oliver heard "wrong," but didn't comment. They ate in silence until Liberty finished her beans.

"Any idea what could make the water do that?" she asked.

"The source is a local well?"

"Yes."

Oliver pulled out his mobile and did a quick search. "Some type of bacteria, maybe?"

"In other words, I need to find an expert."

"I'd assume so."

Liberty gathered his bowl with hers.

"Allow me to do the cleanup." Oliver took the dishes to the larger sink. "This water looks normal."

"It's city water."

"You have two water sources?"

"The well only serves the old sink. It is connected to the original well dug in 1768 by my ninth great-grandfather Silas Hawthorne. He started the inn." Using one of the flour sack towels, Liberty dried the dishes.

"Then why is it called Covington House Bed & Breakfast?"

"His son-in-law eventually inherited it. Josiah Covington."

"Ah, my room's namesake." Oliver wiped down the sink as it drained.

"He married Lavinia Hawthorne."

"The one who cast a spell on the British?"

"Not exactly on them—there was a very convenient fog. Some people claim Lavinia caused it. Others point out it was late spring, and the fog could have been natural." She reached around him to put the ladle away before her arm brushed his side and they both froze. The ladle clattered across the floor.

"I got it," said Liberty.

"Allow me." Oliver's arm tangled with Liberty's as they reached for the ladle and his feet slipped out from under him. Liberty followed him down, landing on his legs.

Oliver's hand hovered over her right shoulder. "Did I hurt you?"

She shook her head and slid off his legs to the floor. "No, I had a better cushion this time. Are you going to make a habit of knocking me off my feet?"

"I don't usually." Oliver stood and offered a hand to Liberty. When she stood, she was closer than he expected—close enough he could see the flecks in her eyes. Their gray-blue reminded him of the sky when a storm cleared. Liberty returned his gaze for a moment, "I didn't hurt you when I landed, did I?"

"Not at all." Oliver wasn't sure if he should step closer or step away. Although only their hands touched, he was aware of every inch of her, as if some unseen current connected them.

The front door slammed. Oliver had an unobstructed view of the back side of the reception desk. He stepped back. Over Liberty's shoulder, he looked for the person who intruded on their moment.

Zetta.

"There you are, babe. I've searched everywhere for you."

# Chapter 10

*U*ntil a few weeks ago, headaches had only been metaphorical to Liberty. Sure, she kept a supply of travel-size ibuprofen bottles for guests to purchase. However, the pounding, squeezing pain had not been part of her understanding. The headache Liberty suffered this morning was accompanied by the drowsiness of a sleepless night and a feeling of loss.

Thank goodness Dean returned as Oliver's girlfriend started yelling. Grandpa sent Liberty into the family quarters, saying he would close up for the night. She took the offered escape. How could Oliver flirt with her when he had a girlfriend? Not that Oliver did anything other than stand there holding her hand for a few seconds longer than necessary. It wasn't his fault that her heart kicked into high speed every time he was near. She was probably only hyperaware of him because he was a Brit and the whole Brit lecture from the cousins.

She knew she should have stayed away from Brits.

Maybe she should stay away from *men*. She'd tried falling for her best friend several times. It never worked out. Her male friends always fell for someone else and used her as a sounding board. Greg was the only friend-boy where things ended amicably. Perhaps because they'd been so young when she had tried to get him to fall in love with her, they honestly had become friends. Proving she couldn't force friendship or romance. Grandma Tansy always told everyone there was no such thing as a love potion and no way to make anyone love you. Just as well. Greg was better as a friend, anyway. It helped that Liberty silently supported Greg's interest in choosing her cousin Josie, even if Josie hadn't figured it out yet.

The calendar on Liberty's wall reminded her she only had three weeks left until the reunion and only two until the guests started arriving. Liberty checked the weather app on her phone. Still sunny with a few clouds. Good, it would be a perfect day to paint the things she hadn't contracted out. Too bad she'd lost the help she'd recruited so easily last night. As long as the goat didn't help, it shouldn't be too bad.

Liberty rolled out of bed and put on her oldest stained jeans and shirt. How people painted without getting paint on them baffled her. Dad once told her she was a paint magnet. If she spilled a drop of paint, it would end up on her. By the end of the day, the sling would have red and white drips on it. The thought of keeping her arm in a plastic bag wasn't pleasant. If only there was a spell to keep things clean. Only she didn't have any magic as her cousins did.

Neither Keira nor Makenna could cast a spell to clean the house or knit bones together or get rid of a cold. Still, they could do something. There was no denying there were elements of magic in what they did. It wasn't the black-hat-wearing, cauldron-stirring, spell-casting magic she'd dreamed of having as a kid.

Not that she'd shown any sort of anything akin to magic. Keira was a couple of years younger, and she had some.

But then Claire was older, and she didn't have any either. Liberty suspected that Grandma Tansy had more than her share. But even her herbs and oils couldn't heal a broken shoulder bone. Although they had made the cold bearable.

Liberty slipped on her shoes and went down to the small kitchenette in the residence to grab a yogurt and some granola before going out to paint.

The day was gorgeous, as the forecast predicted. After chaining the goat in another area, Liberty started with the goat shed. Billy was too curious for his own good. If cats had nine lives, goats had to have ninety.

Painting with her left hand wasn't as hard as she expected until she got to the corners. The control she normally had over her brush wasn't the same as her right. To get into the corners, Liberty felt like she was twisting her wrist backward.

*Plop.* The first of the day's big paint drops fell on her knee. Liberty blotted it with an old towel and tried again. Twenty minutes later, the corner looked like a group of kindergartners had painted it. Liberty sighed and wiped the back of her hand across her forehead and moved onto the second side. Halfway through, she dropped the brush into the paint can. Using a twig, she fished out the brush. Paint oozed off it.

"That is an interesting way to paint."

Liberty twisted around, dropping the brush again. "Oliver, what are you doing here?"

"Last night, I agreed to help you."

"I thought you left."

He raised his brows. "Obviously not."

"Oh." She couldn't find anything to say.

"Do you have a brush for me?"

Liberty looked at the one that was drowned in the paint. "I have some brushes in the shed. I need a new one too."

Liberty set the paint down and turned to face Oliver.

He pointed at the center of his forehead. "You have some paint…"

Liberty grabbed a towel to wipe it off.

Oliver laughed. "Now you have more. May I?"

Liberty nodded and handed him the towel.

Oliver stepped back from the stained towel. "Perhaps a new towel?"

Liberty looked down at the towel she held. No wonder she got more paint on her face. She felt her face warm. Hopefully, he wouldn't notice it under the red paint. "I guess I spilled more than I thought I did."

"You're right-handed, correct? It can't be easy painting with your left."

Liberty gestured to the half-painted shed. "As you can see, I am not very adept at it."

"At least you won't notice how bad my painting is."

"Hopefully, no one will notice any poor painting." Liberty started down a path but then waited. "Let's find you a brush."

Oliver followed her into a neatly arranged work shed. Liberty stopped to look in a foggy mirror placed above an old sink. Her eyes widened. She turned on the faucet and splashed water on her face. Oliver grabbed her wrist to stop her before she got paint everywhere. With his other hand, he took a clean towel off a shelf. He dampened it under the running water. "Use this. You don't want paint running into your eyes."

"You must think I am an accident-prone klutz."

"Not really. You are attempting to do what most people would put off for six weeks, if not forever, using your injury as a valid excuse. Does a goat shed really need to be painted?"

"I just want the place to look nice. Everyone will wander all over the house and farm as if they own them, trying to find a place to connect with their Covington ancestors. I don't want someone to think I'm neglecting the place. After all, over the years, people have tried to claim that they had a right to live here or stay here for free. They have no clue how many living descendants there are of Lavinia Hawthorne Covington."

"How many is that?"

"Makenna claims there could be over eight thousand living descendants because we are now eight to ten generations out. One-third of Americans can't name all of their grandparents. The only reason the reunion isn't overrun is so few people know their heritage."

"So you could have fifty thousand cousins?"

"It is pretty fascinating when Makenna pulls out charts showing genealogical lines. At least for the first hour. By the third, not so much."

Oliver joined her in laughing. "I only know information on one of my lines. My grandfather is a minor baron. His house is full of paintings of dead barons."

"So are you a Lord then?"

"That isn't how it works. The title is usually passed from father to son. In my case, I have to wait for my grandfather to pass before I get the title, as my father has refused to take it. It could be another twenty years before I get the title."

"Does that mean you are royalty?"

"Not always, but in my case, I am descended from King George."

"Does that mean you are in line for the throne?"

"I have no clue. If I am, it would be probably number 48,376th in line or something. I went to one school Prince Harry did, but he was several years ahead of me. That is as close to royalty as I've gotten."

Liberty checked her face in the mirror. "I am not sure if I still have paint on me or if I got too much sun."

Oliver examined her face. There was just a little paint near her hairline. He ran his fingers across it. "I think you'll need to wash your hair to get this out."

"Not that. Do you know how hard it is to wash my hair?" She stepped back and shook her head. "Sorry, didn't mean to complain. I'm getting better at doing things. I just keep trying to use my right hand to wash my hair. And that doesn't work out well."

Offering to wash her hair crossed Oliver's mind. Her hair was soft, although the short strands looked like they would be spiky. "Maybe one of your cousins could help you."

"I have an appointment for a trim Monday. They'll wash it thoroughly then. If there is still paint, I'm sure she'll get it out." Liberty walked to a shelf on the opposite side of the shed and picked up several brushes. "Take your pick." On the way back to the goat shed, Liberty didn't walk as close to him. Had he overstepped his bounds by touching her face? Last night he thought they might have something— until Zetta came in.

They reached the goat shed. "Do you want to paint red walls or the white trim?"

Oliver didn't want to hurt her feelings by pointing out that given the drips and uneven strokes on the red walls that the trim might be beyond her current capabilities. "Trim."

As they painted, they discussed the weather and movies. Liberty was unfamiliar with many British actors.

One board near the door looked chewed on.

"Did your goat do this?" asked Oliver.

"Yes. Not sure what Billy thought was the point of doing that. He was only a year old. Mitzy got mad at him for eating her house and took a bite out of his shoulder."

"You have more than one goat?"

"Usually. Goats are naturally herd animals. They don't do well alone. Mitzy is close to giving birth to twins. And I can't help with a birth right now, so I have asked a friend to keep her until after the babies are born."

"So Mitzy and Billy are a family?"

"Pretty much. I am not sure how much goats think of each other as family. I usually sell off the kids in the late fall."

"Why do you keep goats?"

"Natural lawn mowers as long as they are tethered well. They are easier to keep than cows for the historic farm portion of the property. I don't get much milk with only one doe. I sell it to a neighbor to make cheese."

"You mow your lawn with goats?"

"Not all of it. Get them too close to the garden or the flowers and they'll demolish the place." Liberty moved to the last side.

"What other animals do you have?"

"I had a few chickens, but a dog got into the coop last fall. I'm purchasing some chicks to be delivered the first week of May. I didn't need them here with the reunion. Ducks come and stay at the pond, but I don't raise them. I had a pig one year. I might get another, but I found the animals took too much time away from the B&B. And if you aren't serious about raising them for profit, they are money pits."

"And here I thought farm animals were helpful."

"They are if they aren't at a semi-pet level." Liberty painted for another moment. "It isn't any of my business, but what happened last night?"

"With my driver?"

"She is your driver?"

"Was. I had her transferred this morning. She took the instruction to watch out for me too much to heart. It was more like being stalked. She wasn't raised in Boston, so she couldn't tell me much about the area. I talked my uncle into letting me use local ride share drivers who could give me information about the area." There had been more to the conversation as Oliver had detailed Zetta's behavior over the last several days. The rest of the meeting went well enough. Uncle Pierceton wasn't thrilled with any of the locations Oliver found. Oliver still smarted over the comment that he needed to be more creative and find new angles.

"She stalked you?"

"Even put something on my mobile, which is how she found me."

"Is that legal?"

"Not sure about laws in the States, but I didn't want to cause any problems. So, I just requested she return to her job in New York."

"That was kind of you."

More like acting in self-preservation. Oliver finished the trim on his side and moved to finish the last side. "This might look too fancy for old Billy to call home."

"As long as there is food, there is nothing too humble or too fancy for a goat."

They laughed together as they finished the shed.

# CHAPTER 11

*L*iberty sat on the back porch swing, exhausted. With Oliver's help, she had accomplished more over the weekend than she imagined she could.

The back door creaked. "There you are." Grandpa sat down beside her. "The place is looking nice. Those Monroe boys have been a big help. Looks like you even got your British friend to work for you."

"He offered."

"Not a bad guy, is he?"

"Not for a Brit."

"You and your Brits. You can't judge everyone by King George."

Liberty laughed. "The cousins already gave me that lecture."

"I kind of like him," Grandpa said, ignoring Liberty's comment. "If he hadn't hit you driving on the wrong side of the road, I might try to play matchmaker."

"Grandpa." She rolled her eyes.

"Hey, I need a great-grandson. My brother Luke has been saying this place should be passed on to his son since I no longer have a son."

"But you had one."

"But my son didn't have a son."

"He had me."

Grandpa patted Liberty's knee. "I couldn't ask for a better granddaughter, but this place has always passed from father to son. If Michael were alive, I would have already turned the place over to him."

"But Dad isn't alive. Why can't you let me inherit?"

Grandpa rubbed his chin. "It's never been done. A woman has never inherited the inn. When Silas Jr. was killed in 1779, Lavinia's father gave the place to Josiah, not to his daughter."

"But laws were different a hundred years ago. I'm not sure what they were here, but in most places, a woman couldn't own property independent of her husband." Liberty struggled to keep an even tone.

"I'm not sure you can take care of this place alone. After all, it didn't pass on to the next generation until the son was married. Mostly, so he'd have a wife to cook and help."

Liberty tried not to roll her eyes.

"Is marriage a requirement?"

Grandpa rubbed his chin again. "I don't rightly know. I don't even know if there's anything written about how the property passes on."

"So there is nothing legal?"

"My dad just went into the attorney and signed the deed over to me when he was in his sixties. Simple as pie." Grandpa looked over the backyard. "There might be something up in the attic or maybe over at the historical society."

"I wonder if Makenna has anything in her books." They hadn't looked for that the other day when they were searching for information on the well. But then, they hadn't been looking for information on the house.

"That would be a good place to start. I'll go through some of those old papers in the attic."

"So you will give this place to me?"

"No, I'm not giving the house to you."

Liberty blinked to hold back the tears that suddenly sprung to her eyes

"If you get this place, it is because you earned it." Grandpa stood and walked into the orchard.

Earned it? If she hadn't earned the B&B by now, she never would. She had nothing else to give. Ever since her father died, all she'd done was work for the B&B. Even her hospitality management degree was for this old house.

Oliver stepped out of the warm shower. He'd never worked as hard in his life as he had the last two days with Liberty. He worked out in the gym, but that was different. Growing up, he'd had a few chores like keeping his room clean, but there were landscapers to do the mowing and housekeepers to do the cooking and cleaning. Even at work, he didn't do much—just followed the formulas and let the people below him do the hard things so he could do the fun stuff, such as building a resort in Florida.

He'd promised Liberty that if they finished all the painting and repairs she had on her list, he would take her to dinner. Liberty chose a Thai restaurant in Worcester. Not what he expected, but she guaranteed the food was worth it.

Over the years, he'd taken many women to dinner all over the world to pass the time or to have company when eating. Yet, he hadn't felt this nervous about a dinner in years, and it wasn't because he only had one shirt to choose from.

This time, he was more interested in the woman than the food.

He found Liberty in the library. She wore a soft cream sweater and black pants, both devoid of the paint splatters he'd become accustomed to seeing her in. She stood as he entered. "I hope you don't mind—since neither of us can drive, I invited Makenna and Quin along."

"Better than an unknown driver."

Liberty looked at her phone. "Good, because they're in the parking lot."

Oliver escorted her to the car and helped her into the back seat. He exchanged greetings with Quin and Makenna.

Makenna turned toward them. "I haven't been on a double date in forever."

"This isn't exactly a date." Liberty glared at her cousin.

Makenna smiled back.

"Have you been to Worcester before, Oliver?" asked Quin.

"No. But I am surprised you pronounce the name the same way we would in England."

Makenna laughed. "Most Americans don't pronounce it *Wu-ster*, they say *War-chest-er*, or mangle the word. One way we tell who the tourists are. Some linguists claim we speak English much closer to how the language was spoken two hundred years ago in England than you do."

"I read that someplace. Liberty already teased me for dropping the 'T' from British." Oliver deliberately left the consonant out of the word.

Makenna was a wealth of interesting historical tidbits. She sprinkled them into the conversation as Quin drove. The exterior of the restaurant didn't look like much, but inside, it smelled of basil and other spices.

As they waited for dessert, Makenna pulled out her phone. Quin looked at the screen and ducked his head.

Liberty shook hers. "No, Makenna."

"Oh, it will be fun. I've never played family tree with a Brit before."

Oliver looked nervously at his companions, hoping for an explanation.

"I told you Makenna is a genealogist. She enjoys playing

games where she discovers what famous people everyone is related to." Liberty waved her hand as she talked.

Makenna handed over her phone. "If you will fill in your name and your birth date and place, we can see if my genealogy app can find you. Sometimes you'll need to put in your parents' information as well."

Oliver typed in the information, not entirely sure it wasn't some scam, but he decided to trust all three people at the table with him. He handed the mobile to Makenna who tapped a few times.

"Oh, wow, look at this. You are sixth cousins twice removed to Queen Elizabeth. Oh, and a descendant of—" Makenna looked at Liberty.

"King George III. He already told me." Liberty turned to Oliver and smiled. "We can still be friends as long as he doesn't pull a musket on me."

The server delivered their fried banana roti.

Makenna studied her phone. "Oh, you are also related to Charles Dickens and Winston Churchill. And—" Makenna looked at Liberty. "—Willoughby Pitt."

Liberty gasped.

Quin shrugged, as confused as Oliver. "Who is Willoughby Pitt?"

"He was the captain of the British soldiers who were camped at Hawthorne Inn until the day before Lexington and Concord," said Makenna.

"His company of fifty was lost in the fog created by my great-grandmother Lavinia." Liberty turned to Makenna. "Did Willoughby get married?"

"Yes, to a woman named Mary Hill. Not Katherine. They had four children, one of which is Oliver's mother's fourth great-grandmother."

"So I am related to the man that—" Oliver wasn't sure what to ask.

"Lavinia defeated?" Makenna set her phone on the table. "Apparently so. I'm glad to know he had some sort of happy ending though."

Liberty nodded in agreement. "I wonder if he ever saw Katherine again."

Makenna shook her head. "I don't think so. I looked up the area Willoughby was from and there was a Katherine Brown who married in September 1775. She died in childbirth the following year. Willoughby didn't sail for England until March 1776, so I don't think he saw her again."

Both women blinked back tears. Quin pulled out a tissue and handed it to Makenna. "Can you fill us in?"

Makenna wiped her eyes. "The other day I found some letters between Willoughby Pitt and a woman named Katherine. They were engaged or promised. But because of the getting lost in the fog incident, her father forced her to marry someone else. Willoughby was demoted and then injured at Bunker Hill. Eventually, he was sent back to England. After reading the letters, we felt sorry for him. I don't think Lavinia meant to hurt anyone with the fog…"

"Reading the letters made me think differently about the captain. I never thought of British soldiers as having lives too," said Liberty.

"Are you two feeling guilty for a fog that may or may not have been magic?" Quin asked.

The women nodded.

Quin raised an eyebrow and shrugged, implying he didn't understand either.

"Assuming your great-grandmother had magic, she could have done a lot worse things than getting a bunch of soldiers lost in a fog. She didn't take any lives. I consider that a very clean win. I think you two should be proud. I'm glad she didn't blow them up or something."

"The story is still sad, though. Since you are a descendant of Willoughby, we should give you the letters and the canteen we found with them. The canteen is museum quality. I don't know enough to figure out if it belonged to Willoughby or not." Makenna looked to Liberty to concur with her suggestion.

"Maybe he was happy with his wife. They had three children, and I never heard of him, so there must not have been any nasty ghost stories or anything like that," said Oliver.

Makenna straightened. "You have ghosts?"

"I'll tell you about them on the way back to Hawthorne."

Oliver opened her door and walked Liberty into the B&B. The clock in the hall chimed nine.

Oliver stopped at the bottom of the stairs. "It's still early. We could play a game or something."

He didn't want the evening to end either? Liberty's heart sped up a bit as she thought of options. "We keep board games in the library. Or we can find something on TV."

"Games. Easier to talk when we aren't competing with actors."

As she expected, no guests sat in the library. Liberty opened a cupboard. "Choose a game."

Oliver looked over the selection "Monopoly, for a long game. Draughts—I mean, what you call checkers—for a short one."

"So are you trying to figure out if I want to be with you for a long time or a short time? I could choose a middle-length game."

"Then I'd never know. Or you could choose chess, and we wouldn't have to talk to each other at all—just stare each other down."

103

Liberty reached for a box containing one of her Christmas presents. "Tempting, but not very fun. Have you ever played *That's so Clever?*"

"No, is it hard to learn?"

"Not really. It's a dice game that is part luck, part skill, medium length with time to talk. Are you the type of person who needs to read the rules or take my word?" Liberty set the box on the corner table.

"Not that I don't trust you, but I am a reader."

Liberty handed him the rules so he could look over them while she found pencils for the scorecards. Oliver caught on to the game quickly, and soon they were on their second round because Oliver insisted on a best two out of three.

"How long do you think you'll be in Massachusetts?"

"Not sure. Uncle Pierceton has hinted he wants me to see this entire project through from land purchase to grand opening. So far he's liked none of the properties I've shown him, but they're the type of properties we normally buy."

"So nine months, give or take."

"Maybe. I don't know. I almost thought my uncle was going to pull the plug on the project. My cost estimates are more than we budgeted. What about you? Is the B&B your future?"

"I don't know. I hoped so, but my great uncle is trying to convince my grandfather he can't pass it on to a woman. And there is the entire making-a-profit thing. Between competing with the hotels—no offense—and all the internet pseudo-B&B rentals, it is hard to keep the place full enough to make ends meet. My costs keep rising because I can't purchase the volume that big hotels do." Liberty wrote her turn's score on the card.

"Aren't you in a cooperative?"

"A what?"

"A group of bed and breakfasts that uses your collective purchasing power to buy at lower prices."

"No." Liberty stopped shaking her dice. "I've never even looked into such a thing. There are a couple of B&Bs that I share overflow with. Not that any of us have had much of that this last year." She tossed the dice and took her turn, earning several bonus points.

"I'd assume there already is one. Ask around or start your own."

"I don't have time for that." She barely had enough time to do everything she needed to do.

Oliver picked up the dice and rolled for his turn. "My putting a hotel in the area won't help you much, will it?"

"It will take away a certain part of my clientele. The ones who want the quiet out-of-the-way places will still look for B&Bs, which is why all the little rent-a-room here or a cottage there are harming my business more than hotels."

"But if we had built in downtown Hawthorne?" Oliver marked down his score.

"A hotel that close would give this old place a mortal wound. Someday, someone will build close to here. It is only a matter of time."

"Then what will you do?"

"No idea. Turn Covington House into a longer-term rental or something." The idea of Covington House not sheltering people scared her. She checked her scorecard. "Last roll."

She won the game, but the conversation felt like a loss.

"Well, you took best two out of three." Oliver put the dice away.

Liberty didn't want to leave but didn't know what else to say. "You'll be here tomorrow?"

"I've paid for the room until Monday morning."

"You've paid for some hotel in the heart of Boston for more days than that and you aren't there."

"True. Are you going to have work for me tomorrow?"

Liberty shook her head. "Grandpa is adamant about Sunday being a day of rest. He read something back in the Eighties about the Soviets trying to find the most efficient work week, and they realized six days on, one day off yielded the best work. As he puts it, the Bible told them that."

"Will you take a walk with me tomorrow and show me your pond?"

"Sorry. I am going to visit my other grandfather with mom."

"Maybe another day?" Oliver stood and offered her a hand. "You'll be back?"

"Only if you want me here."

Liberty searched his eyes. "Yes, I do."

The clock struck midnight in the hall. Oliver took her hand and pulled her closer. "Good night, Liberty." He kissed her cheek and left the room. Liberty stared at the empty doorway. What was she supposed to do with that?

# CHAPTER 12

The ride share driver was more than happy to take the bonus to drive Oliver around for the morning as he met with estate agents at several locations. The first was an existing hotel that might earn a two-star rating on a good day. As the tour concluded, Oliver wished for a shower to wash off whatever bugs he might have picked up walking through the corridors. The location was decent, but there wasn't a single thing about the property that could be salvaged. Oliver pictured workers in HAZMAT suits cleaning out the place. The next two properties, an old factory and a burned-out warehouse, weren't much better.

Oliver stopped by his hotel room in downtown Boston and gathered his things, checking out for the week. Dean had assured him there was room at the B&B for another two weeks before every female Covington descended upon the city. "It might be a good week to stay elsewhere—perhaps Vermont or New Hampshire. And if you find a place, take me with you." They'd laughed over the statement, but there had been a hint of fear in Dean's eyes.

Oliver hoped he could find more ways to help. Mostly so he'd have an excuse to stay near Liberty.

The last stop was a property on the border of Concord. A British-owned hotel near the site of the first defeat of the redcoats in the colonies held a certain amount of irony. Liberty would probably not approve. Oliver was tempted to purchase the land on the spot because it would annoy the woman. She had such fire and passion when she was upset. Her eyes glowed as if she were a medieval dragon. Yes, she could be fierce as a dragon. As much as he liked seeing that side of her, he didn't want to unnecessarily cause her pain.

The estate agent asked Oliver something. Oliver pushed Liberty out of his mind and asked him to repeat the question.

Soon after 3 p.m., Oliver had the driver let him off in the center of Hawthorne. The chamber of commerce was still open. Oliver hoped Quin had an opening in his schedule.

As luck would have it, Quin was tacking up a poster in the lobby. "Oliver, I didn't know you were back. You finished your apologies—what's up now?"

"Still looking for a site for a hotel. Nothing I found so far satisfies my uncle. I don't know what he wants from me. I've gone through all the usual steps."

"Maybe he wants something unusual." Quin pointed to his empty office. "I don't have any other appointments today. We could brainstorm something."

Oliver sighed as he took the seat opposite of Quin.

"So what do you want out of a hotel?" asked Quin.

"What do I want?" No one had asked him what he wanted in the business. Procuring a site had always been the same: get land, modify the appropriate floor plan from the twelve base plans Bradford-Stone used, and build the hotel.

Quin waited for an answer.

"I want a hotel that isn't like all the other hotels. I've stayed in hotels in almost every chain the world over. The majority of them are indistinguishable from any other hotel room with a few variations. Every once in a while, there is a themed hotel that is different from the others. Theme hotels have a limited reach. They work great in Orlando and other big resort towns, but not so much here."

"How could a hotel be different?"

"I don't know, something like a B&B. Homey and personal."

"So you want your hotel to be like Covington House, only bigger?"

"Yes."

Quin whistled and shook his head. "That would be a nail in the coffin."

"What do you mean?"

"Right now, B&Bs don't really compete with the hotel clientele, but if you could give a B&B experience at a competitive price…"

"It won't ever happen. I think part of the charm of the B&B are their size. Hotels with less than twenty rooms aren't profitable."

"What else do you want with your hotel?" asked Quin.

"To be in another line of work." Oliver's answer surprised him more than it ever could have surprised Quin.

Liberty looked up from the desk. Finally, the man she'd been waiting for walked in. "Oliver, your driver dropped off your suitcases over two hours ago. I put them in your room." Liberty handed Oliver the key to the Josiah room.

"You didn't lift them up the stairs, did you?"

"Nope, I used the dumbwaiter. Although, my therapist says my arm is getting stronger. It must have been all the extra exercise avoiding paint splatters."

"What are your plans for the evening?"

"I'm on desk duty." Oliver was the only new guest they expected. "And I am trying to figure out how to accommodate the increased numbers for two reunion activities. The five-timers had more RSVPs than they planned on."

"Five-timers?"

"We are grouped by how many times we have been able to attend the reunion in our lives. This will be my second time. I was almost twelve the first time. My cousin Josie was the youngest official attendee last time. We don't count the young children, usually babies, that come with their mothers. Several of the activities are by generation. What I really need is another large event tent, as we have maxed out what they will let us do on the city green. But I can't find one to rent that is affordable. Patriots' Day weekend is too popular, especially with the Marathon. I don't think there is a tent in the entire state I can rent. And the only place I can put one is on the lawn in front of Covington House. I already have one between the house and the barn."

"Have any of the groups responded with low numbers?"

"I almost wish. The sevens are the only one we planned correctly on. And that is because Grandma Tansy knows every single one of them by name." Liberty set down her pen. "I think we are going to have to rent out the elementary school and the high school. Their libraries are comprehensive enough and cafeterias small enough to not feel too huge."

"Would you prefer a tent?"

"Only if the weather is pleasant." How had she gotten into this mess?

"Are you on the planning committee or something?"

"No one ever says no to Grandma Tansy. She asked, and I jumped."

"So you are running the B&B for its largest week and planning where to host other activities?"

Liberty sat back on her stool. "My responsibilities seemed more doable last fall when I was recruited. Some other volunteers resigned because of family emergencies—all excellent reasons. We didn't recruit replacements for them all. I plan small events like weddings here at Covington House, but not events that are for over a hundred and fifty people. I should have taken some classes in large event planning with my hospitality major."

"When did you last take a break from this?" Oliver waved at the computer.

"I don't know. I got the call before lunch."

"Come, take a break with me." Oliver held up a bag she hadn't noticed before. "I got some of those sandwiches you call grinders. We can turn dinner into a picnic of sorts."

Liberty considered the computer screen. The numbers wouldn't change if she stared at them all night, and it was too late in the day to call the school district. "Sure, let me tell Mom I am taking a dinner break and grab my jacket. I'll meet you at the swing on the back porch in five minutes."

Liberty hurried through the employee-only door. Mom and Grandpa were in the family parlor discussing the answer to a game show. "Taking a dinner break. Will you mind the desk?"

"That depends, did our guest check back in?"

"Yes, he did."

"Are you taking dinner break with him?"

"Yes." She answered as she ran up the stairs to her room. She had little time to check her makeup and make sure she hadn't rubbed graphite all over her face or something. On the way out, she grabbed an old quilt.

Oliver sat on the swing. "Good thinking on the quilt. I didn't think you'd want me using one from my room."

"We keep a few old loaners around for this sort of thing."

Liberty chose the path to the pond. "Did you find anything good today?"

"Don't know yet. I need to run some numbers and look at past surveys."

"Welcome to the pond. It isn't much, but I like it here. It's my quiet place." Liberty shook out the blanket with one hand and tried to spread it.

"Trade me." Oliver took the blanket and handed her the food bag. Using both of his hands, he spread the blanket in one quick motion.

Liberty sat so she could see the sunset reflect on the pond—if they stayed out that long. Oliver sat next to her. "I got a couple different kinds of sandwiches. I ordered what I heard other people order and hoped you would like at least one."

"I forgot drinks." Liberty rolled to her knees.

"I have bottled water." Oliver took the bottles out of the bag and set them on the blanket.

Liberty unscrewed the cap. "Thanks for coming prepared."

"I was a Boy Scout."

"They have those in England?" Repositioning closer to Oliver was a gamble, however he was her magnet.

"They started in England. Founded by Robert Baden-Powell, First Baron Baden-Powell."

"What a long name."

"Also known as Lord Baden-Powell. He and his sister also founded the Girl Scout and Girl Guides."

"How did I not know this?"

"Were you a Scout?"

"No." In junior high, track took up all of her spare time.

"Then you probably never learned the history of either organization."

"I always thought the Scouts were so American."

Oliver laughed. "See, not everything British is bad."

"I've changed my mind about most things British over the last three weeks."

"Really?"

"Yes. Makenna pointed out I'd taken things too far. She told me I crossed the line to racist." Liberty ducked her head, not wanting to see Oliver's reaction to her confession.

"And here I thought that glare was because I ran you off the road and broke your collarbone."

Shame filled Liberty, forming a lump in her throat. Tears blurred her vision, obscuring the sandwich wrapper she held in her hands. Oliver moved in front of her, but she still didn't look up.

He removed the sandwich from her hands and replaced it with his own hand. "Liberty?" She liked the way his accent softened her name. "Liberty?"

Unable to resist, she raised her head. Oliver cupped her cheek and wiped a tear with the pad of his thumb. "Don't cry. You already apologized."

"I—I—" Instead of words, only more tears came. Liberty couldn't explain the emotions she felt, the pain of her own stupidity or the joy of befriending the man in front of her. She wept for poor Willoughby and Katherine whose joy was interrupted by war. And for Lavinia's brothers who gave their lives during the Revolution, and her son and youngest brother Thomas who were lost in the War of 1812. Liberty knew their pain in losing her father to a war that wasn't even a war exactly.

Oliver pulled her into his arms and let her cry all over his Oxford shirt. Clarity came as the tears washed away her pain. She never really hated the Brits, she hated the war and the fighting. She'd been writing the essay on the Revolution the day that two men had come to the door and told her mother Dad had been killed by insurgents—a generic name for a nearly invisible enemy.

Her tears slowed, and she became more aware of the powerful arms encircling her and the warm hand rubbing her back. Great, she'd ugly-cried all over a man she liked well enough to find herself checking in the mirror to make sure her face was clean. Liberty enjoyed his embrace a moment more before lifting her head from his chest.

"Tissue?" Oliver held a paper restaurant napkin between his fingers. "Sorry, much to Mum's dismay, I'm not one of those men who has a handkerchief at the ready."

Liberty took the napkin and turned away as she wiped her eyes and blew her nose. If she was going to have to embarrass herself in front of a man, at least she was doing it with one who would be out of her life in a few months. That must be the lure of a vacation romance—all of the embarrassing parts would be forgotten.

Liberty wadded up the napkin and stuffed it into her pocket, took a steadying breath, and raised her eyes to meet Oliver's. "I'm sorry for that." She waved her hand to the damp spot on his shirt.

Oliver caught her hand. "Don't worry about it. It will dry. What about you?"

"I don't think I ever really hated Brits. It was how eleven-year-old me felt with Dad being killed in Afghanistan. I couldn't understand that war, but living here, the Revolution was so real to me with the reenactments and everything. I took out my pain and anger on something I understood. Or thought I understood. I'm so sorry."

She searched his eyes. He had to believe her because she…

Liberty wasn't sure what she needed, but she knew what she wanted and that was to kiss a Brit.

# CHAPTER 13

The setting sun cast soft shadows across Liberty's face. Even with her red-rimmed eyes, Oliver wasn't sure he'd seen anything so beautiful. It was her soul, her emotions, and her honesty. He could only think of one answer for her apology. She didn't move as he brushed the last remnant of a tear from her cheek. As he moved his hand to the back of her head, her eyes widened and searched his. He lowered his lips to hers and tasted of the salt left from her tears. Softy, he tried to erase them, to accept her as she was, and ask her to accept him. He pulled back and searched her eyes before touching her lips a second time and deepening the kiss, pulling her closer, mindful of her shoulder.

Oliver lifted his head a second time and pulled her into another hug. "I'm glad you don't hate me."

"I never hated you. Although I am still annoyed you don't know which side of the road to drive on."

He pulled back so he could see her face. "Understandable."

"In a very weird way, I'm glad you hit me."

"Are you saying you're one of those people who has to literally be knocked off their feet?"

Liberty's smile lit her entire face. "Maybe?" She pulled back further. "I need to show you my tree."

"Your hawthorn tree?"

"I named her Treebie. I thought I was such a smart ten-year-old." Liberty took his hand and led him part of the way around the pond. The hawthorn wasn't as spectacular as the one in the front yard. Only a few buds bloomed among the new green leaves.

Liberty traced the letters LBC in the bark. "My father carved this when I was ten so everyone would know it was my tree."

"So will your daughters have a tree?"

"I don't know. Only girls born at the house, or like me, at the hospital and brought home to the house, have trees planted for them. So if I am living here and have a daughter, yes. If I am living elsewhere, no."

"You'd move?"

"Only if I must. Like if I don't inherit, and I get kicked out." She stumbled over the words.

Oliver dropped the subject. They'd spoken about her troubles before, and he wanted to keep things upbeat. "So do you believe in magic?"

Liberty walked around the tree. "It is hard not to. When I went to my first reunion, my cousins and I tried to summon magic under a full moon. We broke into the original well, and then made wishes and some truly terrible hawthorn berry tea from some old, shriveled berries we found on Lavinia's tree. Even the birds hadn't wanted those berries. We ended up in a lot of trouble. But recently, things have happened around Keira and Makenna. You've had Keira's scones, right?"

"Yes, they taste just like the ones my mother's cook used to make."

"Only to you. To someone else, a scone from the same batch might taste like lemonade or pumpkin pie. But whatever they taste like, there is always a memory that comes with them."

"So when I pictured sitting in the kitchen of our country house with a plate of scones the way I did when I was seven or eight, it was a memory because of the scone?"

"Since your memory was of another scone, the experience probably wasn't as obvious. I had one taste like lemons and another like the nasty tea we made. I could hardly finish eating, but I remembered details about when my cousins and I wanted to be witches I'd forgotten."

Oliver nodded but didn't comment. A scone is a scone.

"Makenna finds things and matches them to people. I saw her hand a woman an old sewing basket, and the woman broke down in tears talking about her great aunt. Makenna tells about teens who traded their phones to play board games with their parents after she matched them with an old popcorn popper."

"She sold me an old inkwell and penknife, but so far, nothing—other than it's kind of cool, and I make poor quill pens. Quin said something about there being something special when she does that, but couldn't people getting emotional over antiques be coincidental?"

"You are making quill pens because you bought an antique. Isn't that weird?"

"Maybe." He'd purchased old paintings and never had the desire to paint.

"Neither of my cousins are casting spells per se. Although Keira has a cookie recipe that is guaranteed to render the most argumentative of board meetings friendly. It is also wonderful for bridal showers where bridezilla and the mother-in-law-to-be don't get along already."

"So what about you?"

"I'm not sure I have magic, but I think the old well has some healing power. I never had a cold in my life until I stopped drinking the well water daily. Unfortunately, I can't get anyone out here to look at it for almost three weeks. One company told me to pour bleach down the well, but that feels wrong. The new cook threatened to call the city and have my food license pulled if I turned on the water again before I get it fixed. I don't understand why she shut off the water in the first place without telling us."

"The no-cold thing could be a coincidence too."

Liberty nodded. "Maybe. But as we reviewed the old stories. I believe it is a special well. I found a story in one of Makenna's old books about a woman bathing her smallpox scars in the water and the scars disappeared. She ended up marrying into the Covington family. There are several accounts of people coming to Lavinia to have maladies cured. The water was always part of the cure by either bathing in or drinking it. But the details are sketchy. There is one couple that comes here at the end of June every year to celebrate their anniversary. The wife's hands are gnarled with arthritis. By the end of their week here, her hands are always better, and she is walking better. I thought the hawthorn berry tea helped her, but I always make the tea with the well water... The story sounds silly, doesn't it?"

"I'm not sure. I mean, there is a ghost in my country house. Many people think old places are haunted. But if you always had the water, doesn't that mean you always had the magic?"

"Maybe. I didn't realize what I had until it was taken away."

"Few of us realize the good things we have until we lose them."

They leaned their backs against the tree and watched the sunset's last colors fade into twilight. Oliver intertwined his fingers with Liberty's. "And sometimes we find something we don't know how to keep." He turned and kissed her again, pinning her against the tree. Liberty leaned into his kiss, taking what he gave and giving back. Above them, an owl hooted. Oliver ended the kiss. He wasn't sure how he could make it happen, but somehow this needed to be more than a travel romance.

# CHAPTER 11

The physical therapist concluded the last exercise. "You're doing well. You get to graduate to four hours a day without the sling. If that feels good, keep adding a half hour a day. Keep lifting to a minimum. Pillows and light things? Great. Avoid a full gallon of milk. If your shoulder throbs, put the brace back on and give it a break. Ice when necessary."

Liberty looked at the figure-eight bandage still protecting her bone. "I can ditch the brace?"

"Only for four hours." The handsome therapist sternly reminded her with a wink.

"May I drive?"

"Yes, as long as you don't get in any accidents—which is recommended even if you aren't recovering from an injury."

Liberty hopped down from the table and pulled a cardigan over her camisole. Her list for the week just got a lot easier.

Outside of the clinic, Grandpa waited. Several opened letters sat on the center console.

"Good news. I can ditch the sling for part of the day."

Grandpa looked up, but he didn't smile. "That *is* good." He sighed. "Unfortunately, I have some bad news. My nephew

Clifton has threatened to hire a lawyer, saying the B&B is his."

"Clifton. Isn't he the one that spent time in jail for embezzlement?"

"Only six months. But I still don't trust him. Never have since the first time I caught him stealing a biscuit when he was a boy." Grandpa set the letter down and started the car.

"But he doesn't have any legal right to Covington House, does he?"

"I don't know. His father Luke is still trying to pressure me, saying that Clifton needs a career and no one will hire him."

"Does he know the first thing about running a B&B?"

"I don't think so. He helped one summer when he was a teenager. I had to chase him down several times a day. He could climb a tree to smoke but couldn't climb a ladder to change a lightbulb."

"What are you going to do?"

"I think I'll make an appointment with the attorney." Grandpa turned onto the highway. Knowing he didn't like to talk and drive, Liberty didn't ask any more questions.

If ever there was a perfect property for a hotel, this was it. Oliver had found it. Convenient access to a freeway but not so close that the traffic noise would overwhelm the guests. The MBTA commuter rail stop was only three blocks away. The hotel could provide a shuttle van for tourists. A walking trail across the street meandered around protected wetlands. And unlike the Cambridge property, there were no asbestos or other environmental concerns.

Oliver walked around the property again as he listened to the estate agent list the incentives the town would provide. Uncle Pierceton couldn't possibly be dissatisfied with the location. If they were careful with the construction, they could preserve the trees on the south side near a brook which would provide a nice outdoor feature for the guests. For a mid-scale hotel, the property would be perfect. A hundred rooms and a conference area. Oliver took several photos with his camera and paced off the space in the overgrown parking lot.

"Do you have anything more for me today?"

"One more place on the north shore about an hour drive."

Oliver sat in the back seat of the ride share, glad to have the same driver as before. Opening his laptop, he uploaded the photos and started a preliminary presentation.

Liberty parked the van behind Abigail's Antiques next to Makenna's van. Her knock on the back door was met by a faint buzzing sound indicating the electric door unlocked. Liberty wound her way through the store, avoiding the enormous claw-footed armoire that once ate Makenna's skirt. "You need to sell that thing. It gives me the creeps."

Makenna laughed. "Clawfoot has grown on me. But not enough I would dare put the wardrobe in my bedroom."

"That could make for an interesting wedding night."

Makenna blushed to the roots of her hair. "Don't even go there."

"How are your wedding plans going?"

"I should ask you that since we're getting married in your ballroom."

"Ask me on April 21st. Other than scheduling the space and reserving three rooms for the day, I've done nothing."

"Some maid of honor you are." Makenna's teasing tone showed no malice.

"Are you sure you don't want to book the honeymoon suite?"

"And have you know where we are staying? No way. Quin won't even tell me where we will be. I think he is afraid my cousins might cast a spell or something. Hey, your sling is off."

"Just for a few hours. I am loving the freedom, even if I can't do much. I drove over here." Liberty hadn't been so excited to drive since she'd first gotten her license. "And I'll take your change of subject and stop teasing."

"My turn. Is Oliver still at Covington House?"

Liberty tried in vain to squelch the blush she knew was growing on her face.

"You kissed him!"

The bell over the door rang as a customer came in. Liberty widened her eyes at her cousin, hoping she'd take it down a notch.

Makenna shifted her focus. "Ah, UPS. One of my favorite people to see."

The brown-clad driver handed over the package. "Good to see you too."

Liberty waited until the driver exited before looking at her cousin. "I didn't say he kissed me. Don't tell me you can read minds now too."

"I haven't seen you blush like that for years. Of course he kissed you, and you kissed him back. I don't need to be psychic to guess that much."

The bell over the door rang again, and Liberty decided she might as well get to the point so Makenna could work. "I came to borrow the key to your house. I need to look through those old Covington histories again."

Makenna pulled her house key from her apron pocket. "Saved by a customer. I'll be over at lunch for more questions."

Liberty found the books on Hawthorne/Covington history on the coffee table. She flipped through the pages, searching for the dates the Covington House property transferred.

Often the inheritance was only a sidenote to another story, usually involving the well.

Liberty stopped and flipped back to the first story. On a legal pad Makenna left on her coffee table, Liberty took notes.

> Josiah Covington lined the well with new rocks around 1815.
>
> In 1825 Josiah's son built a well house.
>
> About 1860 Josiah's grandson son added a hand pump 1860.
>
> In 1894 Josiah's great-grandson piped the water into the kitchen.
>
> Josiah's great-great-grandson added a motorized pump to make the water accessible for the entire house in 1922.
>
> Josiah's third-great-grandson son replaced the lead pipes with copper in 1951.

There weren't any more records. The next one should have been Grandpa who was the fourth great-grandson.

Liberty dialed Grandpa's number.

"Hey, Lib, what do you need?"

"About the time that Great-grandpa signed the deed over to you, did you do any improvements to the well?"

"Improvements? No. Around '75 the city wanted us to cap the well off and only use city water. I fought to keep the well for Covington House. In the end, we compromised, and we were allowed to keep the old well serving the old sink as long as it didn't need any major upgrades. Suppose they don't want us digging a new one. So, I converted the rest of the house to municipal water. I was in the middle of doing that when my dad signed the deed over to me. Fortunately, my father had already replaced all the old lead pipes before it was fashionable. Why do you ask?"

"I'm trying to figure something out. Did my dad ever do anything with the well?"

There was a pause on the other end of the line. "Not that I recall. We haven't had any problems until recently."

"Thanks, Grandpa."

"Did you find anything about the house?" asked Dean.

"No, nothing saying it even has to pass from father to son. What did you find?"

"A bunch of dusty old papers. Half of them I can't read even with my readers."

"I'll keep looking."

"Bye."

Liberty looked at her notes. What if the inheritance wasn't about the house at all?

# CHAPTER 15

*L*iberty directed her cousins in how to rotate the drying berries. Frozen berries didn't seem to dry any slower than fresh ones did.

"How often do you change the trays?" asked Claire.

"Usually twice."

Keira slid a tray into the top shelf of the five-foot-high dehydrator. "I can't believe you got these berries all on trays to begin with."

"Grandpa helped." Liberty cut a berry in half to see how it was drying.

"Not Oliver?" asked Makenna.

"Oliver?" repeated Josie.

"Oh, look. Liberty is blushing," said Claire.

"Knock it off. I don't hate Brits anymore, and Oliver is helping me see the light."

Makenna laughed. "I believe the British term is snogging."

"You kissed Oliver?" asked Keira.

Josie dropped the spoon she held. "You kissed a Brit?"

Liberty put her hand on her hip. "Yes. We kissed."

Claire stopped what she was doing and scrolled through her phone. "So is he a prince?"

"No, but he is a descendant of King George III." Makenna answered before Liberty could explain. "So he has royal blood, I'll let that count."

Claire read from her phone. "I want to marry my best guy friend or be swept off my feet by a handsome prince." She put the phone back in her pocket. "That is an exact quote from the notes I took that night. I figured I should take photos, since I don't want to carry around the book."

"Oh, he definitely knocked you off your feet." Makenna laughed, and the others joined her.

*Twice.* But Liberty wasn't going to admit that. "You know that isn't what I meant. I wasn't talking literally," said Liberty.

"Maybe he's the one." Josie pirouetted and batted her eyelashes.

"Save the dramatics for the stage, Jo. He lives in England. I don't see how this could work out, even if I wanted a permanent relationship."

Claire sat on the stool in the corner. "You mean you're starting something you know won't end well?"

"Stupid, huh? I've never been someone's vacation romance. And I've always stayed away from guests. I didn't intend to let things go further than friends… They just did."

"When he breaks your heart, come get chocolate." Maple Sugar & Spice, Josie's candy store, had the best hand-dipped chocolate in the area.

"Say 'if' not 'when.' It could work out," said Keira.

"Easy for you to say. You already found your Prince Charming," said Liberty.

Claire studied her phone screen again as she spoke. "Maybe now you'll get your magic. Keira and Makenna's manifested about the time when their wishes for husbands came true."

"Coincidence," said Makenna and Keira in unison.

Liberty latched the last dehydrator door shut. "We've dealt with the Oliver subject enough. I know I shouldn't start a romance that isn't going anywhere. Moving on, I found an odd correlation between Covington House being passed on and the well…" Liberty shared the discovery she'd made yesterday. "Now something is wrong with the well. The water is brown and smells terrible. I think I am supposed to fix it."

"How?"

"I'm not sure. I ordered a water testing kit. Tonight, I am going to get the sample to send to the lab. I think the problem might be iron bacteria. But I have no idea how it started now. I checked the geological map and iron isn't one of the minerals known to be in abundance in the area." A shadow passed by the window. Liberty watched to be sure. It was Oliver. Grandpa must have warned him not to stop in the summer kitchen.

"How do you fix iron bacteria?" asked Josie.

"Chlorine."

"No!" Makenna yelled. "If the water does have magic in it. Chlorine could alter the power."

"I've thought about that. I am hoping to find an answer. If any of you run across any information about the well, or if Grandma Tansy is in a talkative mood, try to get her to spill."

Keira hung her apron on the hook. She had been the only cousin to put one on. "You think Grandma Tansy knows something?"

"Doesn't she always?" answered Claire.

The cousins answered "Yes" in unison, sending them off into another fit of laughter.

Another week, another presentation. Oliver couldn't believe a week had passed since he'd escaped the hotel in Boston. Everything was coming together for him. He'd found the perfect property, a couple of contractors he felt would do the job on time and on budget, and he got to see Liberty every day. With so many business dinners, he hadn't seen her as much as he liked.

She'd been busy too. It had been a pleasant surprise to run into her at the supply closet again this morning. And her quick kiss had been much better than a ratty towel. A comment he'd made the mistake of verbalizing had also earned him a soft slap with her right hand. It was good to see her without her sling, even if it was only "part-time freedom" as she called it.

Oliver finished the slides in his presentation and checked the time.

Liberty had told him she would be down in the old summer kitchen with her cousins. There'd been something in the sentence as well about a dehydrator and hawthorn berries. What mattered was that he wouldn't be able to see her tonight unless he wanted to brave her relatives.

Although he assumed they might know of this improved relationship status with Liberty, he wasn't ready to be with her in front of them—not until he could figure out a way to convince her to come to England. Now she realized Brits weren't the enemy, there wasn't a reason she couldn't live there. Other than Covington House.

Oliver left his room, hoping Liberty was back.

He found Dean at the front desk sifting through old papers.

"Good evening."

Dean didn't look up. "She is still down with her cousins."

"I wasn't even going to ask."

"Yes, you were." Dean stopped shuffling papers and looked Oliver in the eye.

"Eventually."

"What are you doing?" Oliver pointed waving at the large mound of papers.

"Trying to find the logic for passing on Covington House. My nephew has threatened to sue us, claiming he is the current rightful heir. As long as I am alive, he can't do much. But Liberty deserves to run this place."

"Why don't you let her inherit the house?"

"I'm not sure. I keep thinking I should, but it has always passed from father to the oldest son. I need to make sure there isn't a reason." Dean let the sentence hang as he looked over another paper.

"Good luck." Oliver left through the front door. One thing he liked most about Covington House was the freedom to walk around the property to clear his mind. Lights and laughter tumbled out the doors of the old summer kitchen. Oliver avoided the building and turned into the apple orchard. What did Liberty do with all the apples? He judged there were only three acres, but the crop should still be substantial. He found two hawthorn trees at the end of the orchard. Both bore initials. The first tree had a trunk about half again as big as Liberty's tree. The other was almost twice the size. What an interesting tradition. Many people planted trees to commemorate births or deaths but rarely did people keep track of them down generations.

Oliver turned toward the pond and Liberty's tree.

His mobile rang. He looked at the screen twice. "Mum? Is something wrong?"

"Um—" He heard his mother's tears in the single syllable. "Mum?"

"Sorry, Olie, I told myself I'd be composed when I made this call. Maybe I should call back later."

"No. Talk to me."

"I've been visiting with the doctors since you left. I have breast cancer. They scheduled a mastectomy for next Tuesday. If you could possibly come home? Your father—well, as soon as I told him, he went off to London. He doesn't handle stress well. And I want someone at the hospital with me." Father's way of handling stress usually involved getting drunk and sleeping off the problem until he remembered and repeated the cycle for days. That was why he'd retired from the company early. Although, Oliver assumed there was more to the story than that. His father was also the reason Oliver didn't drink. Alcoholism had genetic ties, and Oliver knew he didn't want to follow those footsteps.

"I have a scheduled call with Uncle Pierceton in the morning. I'll let him know the situation. I'm sure he'll let me come back." There was no reason Oliver needed to be in the States to complete the land purchase.

"Thank you so much. I should have asked how business was going over there first." Was it his imagination, or was Mum's voice growing weaker?

"It is about concluded for now."

"That's good. I miss my boy."

"Bye, Mum. Love you."

Oliver emerged from the trees near the pond. It was peaceful. He sat on a stone bench someone had made years ago and looked over the water. As he replayed his mother's call through his mind, he realized he should have asked more questions. What stage was the cancer? How aggressive? What prognosis had the doctor given?

"Someone has stolen my pondering place." Liberty's voice interrupted his thoughts.

"I was hoping you wouldn't mind sharing." Oliver scooted over.

"Is something wrong?" Liberty sat down next to him. Her sling was on again.

"My mother called. She has breast cancer. She wants me home for her surgery."

"When?"

"Tuesday."

Liberty wrapped her left arm around his waist, giving him a half hug. "Have you booked your flight already?"

"No, I need to talk to my uncle in the morning."

She didn't answer but laid her head on his shoulder. They sat that way as the first stars came out.

"Is there anything I can do to help you?"

Oliver wrapped his arm around her, pulling her closer. "Will you write, email, text, video call, whatever? I don't want whatever we have between us to end."

"I don't want it to end either." Her words reverberated through his chest.

Oliver tipped her face up. Liberty craned her neck to meet his lips in a slow, deliberate kiss.

He got lost in her kiss and used her touch to soothe the pain he felt. Oliver stopped, not wanting to take a selfish advantage. "I should get back to my room. I have a 5 o'clock call in the morning."

Liberty ran her hand down his arm, her hand finding his and intertwining her fingers with his. "Mind if I walk you back to the house?"

"No, I'd like the company very much." They walked slowly along the path. If only he could stay with Liberty and be with his mum at the same time.

Liberty stopped at the back porch. "I think I'll go in through the kitchen. I need to test the water."

Oliver didn't want to let her go, but saw the wisdom ending their walk here. "Do you need help?"

"I only need a couple of vials of water."

"Can I find you in the morning and say goodbye?" Oliver stopped in the shadow of the last tree.

"You'd better not leave without saying goodbye."

Oliver bent his head to kiss her again before continuing through the house to his room.

# Chapter 16

*L*iberty checked the clock again. How long was too long for a business call? Oliver said the meeting started at five a.m. That was two and a half hours ago.

There wasn't a *do not disturb* sign on his door, so with an armful of clean towels, she tapped on the door. The world's lamest excuse.

Oliver opened the door and waved her in. His phone was pressed to his ear. He wore his tweed jacket, a tie, and a pair of basketball shorts. Liberty suppressed a giggle since she didn't know who on either end of the phone might hear.

Liberty set the towels down on the chair next to the desk. Her eyes were drawn to the photo on his computer screen. She recognized that area. She ran past that old warehouse often on her morning jogs. The abandoned property sat just over the city line in Weston. She read the bullet points on the screen. Her eyes fell to the scratch pad next to the laptop. A sketch of a hotel room decorated in turn of the twentieth-century furniture, not the normal modern plain stuff. Next to it was a sketch of a room with furniture that almost matched the Josiah room's.

Liberty whirled to face Oliver who listened to his phone, his back to her. He couldn't build there. Not a hotel with charm. It would end her B&B. How could he do that?

Liberty ran from the room and down the back stairs. She burst out of the backdoor, tossed off her sling, and ran.

The call finally ended. He was back in Uncle Pierceton's good graces and had a flight booked to Leeds leaving Logan airport at 2 p.m. Through the window, Oliver saw Liberty run into the orchard. He turned to face his room. She'd been here only minutes ago.

He looked around his room for a clue. His white legs? No, she'd smirked at his shorts. He looked at his desk. The presentation? His doodles of hotel rooms that would never happen in a Bradford-Stone hotel?

Oliver closed his still-open door and exchanged his shorts for pants and rushed outside to find Liberty.

Liberty left a trail through the dewy orchard and fields beyond. Her trail took her over fences and through properties that couldn't belong to the B&B. Oliver hurried to follow the path, hoping no one would yell at him for trespassing. He should have left his shorts on and switched his loafers for trainers. The trail ended at a street. Oliver crossed and looked for any sign that Liberty had continued her cross-country run. A house in the distance looked familiar, as did a partially grown-over driveway. Cautiously, Oliver walked up the drive into a crumbling parking lot for the warehouse, his number one pick for the hotel. But it couldn't be. The property wasn't in Hawthorne.

"This is the place you want to build a hotel, isn't it?" Liberty shouted from the side of the warehouse where she sat in the overgrown weeds. "How could you? Covington House will never survive. And those rooms! You used me, Oliver." She stood and walked in his direction. "I should have known you were too good to be true—my own handsome prince who knocked me off my feet."

"I didn't realize."

"Didn't realize what? That I was falling in love with you? Of course you did. That is how you could use me. Two miles. I only ran two miles."

Oliver reached for her, but she dodged him.

"Don't touch me. Just go home, Oliver. You won. After almost two hundred and fifty years, a Brit won." She took off at a sprint.

"Liberty!" The trees muffled his yell; not even an echo reached him.

Oliver pulled out his mobile and checked the map. What had been two miles over farmland was closer to five by roads? None of them followed the straight line to Covington House. He hadn't realized that Weston was even next to Hawthorne.

Oliver requested a ride share using his app and hoped that Liberty would be calmed down enough to listen when he returned.

Lisa sat at the front desk, a frown on her face. "I understand you are checking out this morning?"

"Yes. I need to fly home. Has Liberty come in?"

"She isn't here. She was supposed to be at a committee meeting ten minutes ago. They are waiting for her in the ballroom, and she isn't answering her phone." Lisa looked to him for answers.

"She was running last I saw her. I thought she would beat me back here."

Lisa's frown deepened.

"If you see her, will you tell her that..." Oliver didn't know what to say. "Tell her it was an accident."

Oliver returned to his room. Liberty's mobile lay on the floor under his desk. She must have dropped it when she ran out. He took the phone back to the front desk and handed it to Lisa. "I found her mobile—I mean cell." He substituted the American term.

"Where?"

"In my room. She saw something on my computer and got upset."

Lisa gave him a mum look. The kind that made a child spill all their secrets. Apparently, those were the same in British and American English.

"I was on the phone arranging my flight back to Leeds. She brought me an extra towel. There was nothing inappropriate." He hadn't had to defend himself like that since Marisa Holmes' father found them snogging in the gazebo when he was fifteen. "I didn't even touch her this morning."

Lisa raised her brows and looked at the clock. "When is your flight?"

"Two."

"It will take you two hours to get to Logan airport this time of day. And another two for international security. You'd better hurry."

Oliver nodded and ran back up the stairs.

Maple Sugar & Spice didn't open until ten. Liberty ran around to the back door and pounded.

Josie opened the door. "Liberty, what is wrong?"

"How much chocolate does it take to fix a broken heart?"

Josie pulled Liberty into her candy-making kitchen. "What happened?"

Liberty sat on one of Josie's step stools. "He used me. He

wasn't a prince after all—just a long-lost relative of that snake, King George."

"I wish I had magic candy that took the pain away. Last time I got dumped, I ate a bunch of chocolate-covered orange rind. Sent my blood sugar sky high. So be careful..."

"How much is too much?"

"Since you aren't diabetic like some of us, if you get sick, stop. Let me give you some of my favorites." Josie opened her walk-in cooler. "Be warned: chocolate will only help for a little while. Cocoa can't solve the problem. Do you want Makenna to come over so you can tell her what is wrong?"

Liberty stuffed a chocolate-covered caramel into her mouth and had to wait a moment before answering. "She had a Friday morning estate auction in Lexington... Besides, I don't want to talk, I want to drown in chocolate."

"Well, you came to the right place." Josie handed her a box. "This is a couple of weeks' worth for me. Don't down them too fast or I'll be jealous."

"You shouldn't be. Although I still wonder why you choose to run the candy store."

"It's part of me. All those years helping mom. I couldn't not run the shop."

"Oliver's mother has breast cancer. He is going back today. After what Aunt Pamela went through, I feel bad for him even though I really want to hate him." Liberty popped a maple cream into her mouth.

Josie wrapped her arms around Liberty. "Do you need an extra pound of chocolate?"

"What I need is time to think. I didn't let him talk, and I should have." Liberty looked at the digital clock on the wall. "Oh, rotten berries. I had a reunion meeting a half hour ago."

"Where?"

"In the ballroom. I'm hosting."

"Have another chocolate before Grandma Tansy tracks you down." Josie handed Liberty another chocolate-covered caramel.

"I don't even have my phone on me."

"Like that will stop Grandma Tansy. When is the meeting over?"

"10:30-ish."

Josie glanced at the wall clock. "I give you ten minutes before you are discovered. I'd tell you to hide out in my apartment upstairs, but we both know she'll find you."

Liberty ate a chocolate cherry. "I should probably run home and face her there."

"Are you going to be okay?"

"Probably. Oliver is flying back to Leeds this afternoon."

"What will you do if you run into him?"

"I'll eat a chocolate and try not to interrupt him while he explains. He was trying to explain, but I can't see a way that this works when his hotel will compete with the B&B and he's even decorating the hotel like Covington House."

Josie gave Liberty another hug. "Tonight, we can do cousins' night at my place. I'll have some popcorn and vegetables to counteract all the sugar."

"Will you tell them Oliver is off limits as a topic and zero jokes about princes?"

"Will do."

Liberty took a long way back to Covington House and wasn't surprised to find Grandma Tansy waiting for her near the summer kitchen.

"I wondered how the hawthorn berry drying was working."

"They looked good last night."

"You missed our meeting." Grandma Tansy shook her finger as she talked.

"I know."

"Good thing I found your notebook. It answered all our questions."

Liberty was sure the book had been in her bedroom. But this was Grandma Tansy.

"I told everyone you had a minor emergency to deal with. I also saw that man of yours get into a car with all his luggage. Would you like to explain?"

*No.* "His mother is ill, and he returned to Leeds."

"So, he'll be back?"

"Not here."

"Liberty Belle Covington. You are being evasive."

"Yes, I am."

Grandma Tansy laughed. "You wanted to tell me I am being nosey. But this is important, and you shouldn't—-" She halted. "Never mind me. I need to go. I should have opened the apothecary by now."

Grandma Tansy hurried around the house at twice her normal shuffle. Knowing it was safe to return to the B&B, Liberty got back to work.

As she reached the front desk, Officer Hastings entered the front door.

"Greg, what are you doing here?"

"I got a call from Mr. Bradford. He said he left something at the desk for me."

Liberty dug around and found an envelope labeled *Police* and another labeled *Fire Department.* "Here you go. Will you drop this one off too?"

Greg turned the envelopes over. "Sure. Do you know what is in them?"

"I didn't even know they were here."

"The envelope is only addressed *Police.* That's me, right?" Greg opened the police envelope and let out a low whistle. "If that guy hadn't already paid his ticket without contest, I would say that he was trying to bribe us. A check to the police officer's widows and orphans' fund." Greg flipped over the cheek so she could see the five zeros behind the first number.

"He can write a check that big?" Was that a business account or a personal one? Liberty had never considered Oliver's finances.

"You didn't know? I thought you were out with him the other night."

"How do you know we were out?"

"Quin passed me where I was doing a traffic watch. I saw you in the back of the car laughing with the guy."

"You're worse than a traffic camera."

Greg bowed. "I better get back on my rounds."

"See you later, Greg."

As soon as he left, Liberty scoured the desk for an envelope for her. Nothing.

# CHAPTER 17

The chair in the surgery waiting room needed extra padding. Oliver studied the map of Massachusetts on his phone for the thousandth time. How could he have missed that his recommendation of a hotel property was practically next door to Covington House? When he showed the satellite map shot in his presentation, the corner of Covington House's pond was in view.

He'd spent the few hours he'd had in the office yesterday trying to convince Uncle Pierceton to go with another property. Even the one in Concord would be better, as it was further away. No decisions would be made until the next planning meeting.

As yet, he hadn't tried to text or call Liberty. First, he wanted good news to tell her with his apology.

The nurse at the reception desk called him and told him to go into consultation room two.

A doctor in clean scrubs came in. "Oliver Bradford?"

"Yes?"

"Your mother asked me to tell you about her surgery. It was successful—" For a moment the words flew past Oliver's ears. "—we will of course be waiting on the biopsy of the lymph nodes to see if the cancer spread. Do you have questions?"

"Not right now."

"I'll have the orderly escort you to her room as soon as she is out of recovery." The doctor left Oliver alone in the room.

Best news he'd heard all day. He wanted to share the news with Liberty, but wasn't sure what to text.

*Mum's surgery went well.* That was the simple part. He typed and deleted a half dozen tries before he was happy with the second part. *I hope you are well. I hope we can talk soon so I can explain. Sorry.*

Shortly after he entered his mother's room, an answering text came.

*— Glad your mother is well. Yes, we should talk. After the 21st? Things are crazy here, and I think our talk won't be short.*

A week? She wanted him to wait a week? Maybe in that time he could get Uncle Pierceton to change his mind.

Liberty checked on another set of guests. Only three rooms were empty, and they would be filled by tomorrow night. Laughter filled the halls above her. Good thing that the family wing was separate from the rest of Covington House, because it was unlikely the giant slumber party in the B&B would end soon. When a pizza delivery man came, Liberty directed him to the dining room and called up to rooms: four, six, and eight to come down for their pizzas. She hurried to check that she'd put out adequate paperware.

Ten minutes later, a driver delivered Chinese, and Mario's delivered grinders. Liberty called up to those rooms as well.

The next person through the door was Grandma Tansy with a bakery box from Sweet Memories. "I brought Keira's cookies. You can thank me later."

"Does she have any with sleeping potions in them?"

Grandma Tansy laughed. "Twenty-six—no, thirty-nine years ago, I stayed up four days straight, reconnecting with all my cousins. Sleep when you can. Have fun the rest of the time."

At the desk, things were relatively quiet for the next hour. Grandpa came in from the kitchen. "Go eat while I deal with the horde, but be back in an hour. You have mail in your room."

"Thanks. Everyone scheduled to check in tonight has. It's mostly dealing with food deliveries now."

"I can handle that. Did I see Tansy?"

"Yes."

Grandpa looked heavenward and muttered some unholy words. "Hurry back."

In the family kitchenette, Liberty tossed leftover chicken and dumplings from Sunday into the microwave. She'd asked mom to make a double batch as they were her favorite comfort food. While dinner reheated, she went up to her room and found an envelope from the water lab on her bed.

The good news was that, other than the iron bacteria, the water was safe. No lead, no weird chemicals. Just iron. Which was also the bad news.

While she ate, Liberty looked over the geological survey. Iron wasn't common in this part of the state. How had iron gotten into the well, and how could she remove it? The big question was—would adding chlorine to the water hurt the well?

Liberty found Grandpa watching the grandfather clock. "I don't think you can make time move any faster."

"You're back. They broke out the popcorn. In the main kitchen."

"Fiona isn't going to like that. Thanks for letting me eat dinner."

"What was in the big envelope?"

"Water report on the well. I'll have to get someone out here next week. Fortunately, the taint isn't poisonous. The water only looks bad and smells worse."

"Is the problem fixable?"

"It should be."

"Good girl. I'm going up to my room and removing my hearing aids. If anyone asks, I'm not here." He kissed Liberty on the cheek.

"Don't you tell the girl to lie for you, Dean." Grandma Tansy stood at the dining-room door, her arms crossed.

"It isn't a lie." Grandpa pointed to the desk. "I am not here."

"Fine, go hide in your room." Grandma Tansy crossed to the reception desk and lowered her voice to a whisper. "I made sure every one of them ate at least one bite of Keira's cookies. Even the ones on a diet. It should keep some of the rivalry to a minimum tonight."

Liberty whispered back a thank you.

"Did I hear you mention water?"

"Yes. The well has some iron bacteria in it. Nothing dangerous, just ugly and smelly. I'll get it cleaned and repaired next week."

"Good girl. About time you take care of the well. I'll be back tomorrow." She turned, but then stopped. Out of her bag, she pulled a small jar. "You have a rash on your arm, probably from the sling. This will help."

Liberty attempted to turn her right arm so she could check, but the pain near her collarbone stopped her. She took the cream. "Thank you." Liberty rubbed her thumb across the jar's lid. Her great aunt that everyone called grandma seemed to know a lot about what was going on. "Grandma Tansy? What do you know about the well?"

Grandma Tansy smiled and waved as she exited. There had to be something she knew.

# CHAPTER 18

Oliver checked on his mum before going downstairs to the table he'd set up as his home office. Uncle Pierceton had excused him from coming into the meeting in person. Oliver hoped he could make a good enough argument to talk the planning committee out of the property near Covington House. After reconsidering all the properties, Oliver presented the Cambridge property with T access that he had previously dismissed. Among other things, the asbestos clean-up would not be as costly as he'd thought since there were government grants to businesses that made properties environmentally safe.

This week, Oliver was fully dressed for the meeting—including pants.

The familiar tone of the call starting filled his headphones.

After preliminaries, Oliver had his turn. "Last week, I presented a beautiful property with my recommendation. This week, I would like to present one that has more potential, and I rescind my recommendation for the last week's property in Weston."

Gasps echoed through his headphones.

Oliver ignored them and started his slides. "Initially, I didn't think this property would be viable as it requires the cleanup of asbestos. However, I have learned that there is a government grant available for such cleanup. The property would also support a three hundred-room hotel instead of a ninety-room. Located in Cambridge…" Oliver continued his sales pitch, showing the advantages of the Cambridge property. When he concluded, he opened the presentation to questions.

The first several were expected, including the clarification of surveys and such.

Uncle Pierceton leaned forward and straightened his tie. Everyone waited for his question. "What is the real reason you don't want us to go ahead with the Weston property?"

Oliver looked straight into his computer camera. "When I made the presentation last week, I was not aware of the economic impact the property would have on the town of Hawthorne. After all the trouble we inadvertently caused there last December and January, I believe that having a hotel that close to Hawthorne would hurt their economy in the long run." Oliver pulled up a map. "By car, you can see the hotel is several miles from the Hawthorne town square. However, as the crow flies, the property lays barely two miles from the Covington House Bed & Breakfast. A hotel would pull revenue from Hawthorne without giving anything back, as the local tax revenue would go to the city of Weston."

Uncle Pierceton nodded and looked around the boardroom. No one had more questions. "Oliver, since you are retracting your previous recommendation, which is highly unusual, I am going to excuse you from the rest of the discussion and decision process."

Oliver's screen went black. He threw his head back in frustration, wanting to scream but not wanting to upset his mum. Oliver checked with the housekeeper before escaping to the patio. Rain drizzled down as per usual in mid-April.

He ignored the shower and ran for the gazebo where he could let out his frustrations. Was it wrong to pray that the board listened and chose another property—any other property than Weston?

The check-in line for the second-time group was longer than Liberty expected. So far, there were twenty more people than had preregistered. Liberty handed a freshly printed ID badge and itinerary to the woman she'd been helping, and turned her focus to the next woman in line. "Eden?"

"I didn't think you would recognize me."

"How could I not? And happy birthday! We hoped you would come." Liberty hopped out of her chair to hug her cousin.

"We?"

"Claire, Keira, Makenna, Josie, and I of course."

Eden hugged her back.

"Ouch, careful of the shoulder. I should have worn my sling."

"You're hurt?"

"Almost healed. Broken collarbone." Liberty sat down. "You didn't preregister, did you? We've been watching for your name." Liberty typed Eden's name into the computer. "Is your last name still Noyes?"

"Yes."

Liberty hit print and gathered the rest of the papers. "Where are you staying?"

"Grandma Tansy's."

Liberty added a note to the itinerary on Sunday night. *Reunion at the well, 10 p.m.*

"Be sure you come to this if you skip every other event." Liberty tapped her note to make sure Eden saw it.

"Where will I find the others?"

"Until the opening ceremony at the high school, they're all working. Claire is at Red Leaves Books, Keira is at Sweet Memories Café and Bakery, Josie is across the street at Maple Sugar & Spice, and Makenna is at Abigail's Antiques." Liberty glanced at the line. "We have so much to catch up on! Promise I'll see you again?"

"Promise." Eden disappeared into the crowd, and Liberty turned her attention back to the line of attendees yet to check in.

By the time she finished with registration, the opening ceremonies were more than half over. Liberty took one look at the crowd in the gym and headed back to Covington House. She needed more chairs in the ballroom and a few moments of silence. Since she helped plan the opening ceremonies, she wouldn't miss anything.

Her phone pinged. Oliver.

*— We will build the hotel in Cambridge. I can't wait to talk on the 21st.*

Liberty took a moment to process the text.

*Thanks for letting me know.*

On the way home, she stopped at the market to pick up an extra supply of ibuprofen to fight the forming headache. On the way to her car, she bumped into Trina Hughes.

"Sorry, Liberty. I was looking at my phone. I got a full-price offer for that old warehouse in Weston. I thought it would never sell."

"Really? Who's the buyer?"

"Somebody out of England. The same people who were involved with that mess in January. I better hurry."

Weston was definitely not Cambridge. Liberty's headache grew. Why had Oliver lied?

# CHAPTER 19

By Sunday night at ten, Liberty wasn't sure if she was coming or going. If not for her mom kicking her off of desk duty, she never would have made it to the well to meet her cousins. Her cousins had covered the area with a small 10 x 10 event tent. A low-watt battery-powered lantern lit the space, leaving most things in shadow.

"There you are." Makenna pointed to the last chair. "It looks like rain, and there weren't a lot of places to move our meeting to—my house is stuffed to the seams. I've almost resorted to sleeping in the hidden room."

Eden looked a bit confused.

Claire raised her hand. "I've only caught Eden up on the basics." She turned to Eden. "It'll make sense when Keira and Makenna catch you up on what's happened with them." She glanced over at Makenna. "Just make sure to include the secret room." Her gaze then went to Liberty. "And you need to explain about the well—and your cold."

Keira started with Thanksgiving and the recipe that sent Aunt Ginger to the hospital. "Ginger's fine, now, of course, but it was alarming at the time." She passed around a plate of her memory scones while she gave Eden a quick rundown on them. "I didn't make these for the bakery this week. I am not sure I want everyone at the reunion trying to figure out what is happening. But I have made hundreds of the calming cookies at Grandma Tansy's request."

Makenna took her turn to explain what was going on with the antiques and Quin's experience with the watch. Both of them downplayed Grandma Tansy's role. Liberty understood why. Eden had hung back on the weekend. It wasn't exactly the time to say, "We think your grandma is losing her marbles."

"So are you two the only ones with magic?" asked Eden.

Claire looked for Liberty to answer.

"Well, I may have been interacting with magic all along in a way. Turns out, the well water really is magic. Until a month ago, I'd never had a cold in my life." Liberty told the story of her month, leaving out the romance with Oliver. "So I feel I am supposed to fix the well—like I am more of a caretaker than anything."

"In a way, that's all I am," added Makenna. "But you left out the most important part. Oliver. See, Eden, both Keira and I fell in love about the time our magic started manifesting. Not that we were in love first, just near the same time. What Liberty left out was Oliver, the driver of the car who hit her the first day she had the cold. I've never seen her so in love in her life. And though it's hard to tell because she is so busy this week, she is moping around Liberty-style—which is too busy to think."

"That isn't fair. I am not moping. Besides, he lied to me again."

"When?"

"I got a text from him Friday saying they were building in Cambridge. Not five minutes later, I ran into Trina, and she says she sold the warehouse in Weston to the same company that tried to build a hotel on Makenna's block. So magic or not, Oliver is out of the picture. I'd have a better chance with Greg Hastings if we go back to my original wish, but we all know he doesn't like me."

Claire, Keira, Makenna, and Liberty all looked at Josie.

"No, no, no. He is my best friend's older brother. He doesn't think I am pretty at all. And he is always calling me Squirt, or Little Bit, or something like that. As far as he is concerned, I'm still twelve years old and having my first diabetic emergency. Now that his sister is off and married, he wants to baby me."

Liberty rubbed her arm where it itched. Grandma Tansy's ointment had helped for a while, but now the itching only seemed to get worse. She couldn't wait for the water to get back to normal so she could have her immunity back. Oliver was right about not appreciating something until it was gone. Liberty rubbed harder, hoping the itching would send Oliver out of her brain. She pulled out her jar of ointment and put some on. The relief was immediate.

Eden leaned forward, eyes squinting. "What is that you rubbed on your arm?"

"Something Grandma Tansy gave me the other night. The salve helped for a while, but now my rash is getting worse."

"Have you tried an antihistamine?"

"What is that?" Liberty returned the jar to her pocket. Everyone stared at her. "Sorry. Until a month ago, I'd never even had a cold."

"It's a medication, some of them over the counter, that comes in both pill and lotion form. It helps with allergies," Eden explained. "May I see the ointment Grandma gave you?" She held out her open palm, and Liberty handed over the jar.

Eden opened the ointment and sniffed. "Hmm. I'll bring you something better in the morning. I don't think you should use this anymore."

"I can't wait for the well to get back to normal." Liberty barely held back a sigh. "I want to know if the water really does heal."

Josie's feet dangled above the ground. The standard camp chair was too tall for her. "Explain what the problem is. I didn't understand the first time."

"I got the tests back the other night. There are iron bacteria in the well. The water is safe to drink—no one will get sick—and the bacteria makes the water this ugly orange color and the water stinks like rotten eggs. The odd thing is, according to the geological surveys, we have little naturally occurring iron in the ground in this area of Massachusetts. And it's odd that after over 250 years, the problem could randomly start. If I can find the iron source and remove it, the well may only need to be treated once. They use chlorine, and I am worried an industrial-strength chemical might do something to the water. If only I knew how iron got into the well in the first place." Liberty looked at the cement cover as if it could tell her answers.

"I think I know." Everyone turned at the sound of Josie's voice. "Remember thirteen years ago when we were making the tea and stirring it? It was my turn—I was last, of course. I was stirring a little too hard, and the spoon flew out of my hand and into the well."

They all nodded.

"The spoon was stainless steel," said Josie.

"Which is made of iron," said Claire.

"So it took thirteen years to cause a problem?" asked Kiera.

Makenna reached for another scone. "I assume it would have to oxidize, or rust, before the bacteria formed."

"Iron is magnetic, right?" asked Liberty.

"Yes."

Liberty sat forward excitedly. "I saw online how this man tosses a gigantic magnet into rivers and brings up all sorts of things. If we could get a huge magnet and drop it down the well…"

Keira sat back in her seat holding her hands in the time-out position used by referees. "Oh no, Uncle Dean will kill us if we break into the well again."

"Not if we *fix* the well." Liberty stood and examined the well cover. "Plus, we don't need to remove the cement. We only need the key."

"We still need a magnet," said Josie.

Makenna stood. "I think I have one in the garage. The magnet was in a box of miscellaneous stuff I picked up at the estate sale last month in an all-or-nothing box of things I wanted. The magnet has a long nylon rope and instructions."

Liberty rubbed her hands together. "Let's do this. Makenna, take someone and go find the rope and magnet. After reading about chlorine, I've been nervous to put it in the well assuming the water can heal, however, I don't think a gallon of laundry bleach will hurt it like stronger forms of chlorine. Keira, will you go check the storeroom for bleach? And I'll go talk Grandpa into giving me the key."

Eden checked her phone. "It is after eleven. Will he still be up?"

Liberty stuck her head out of the tent flap. The light in Grandpa's room flickered through the blinds. "I think he's watching TV."

"I can't believe we are doing this again," said Makenna as she followed Liberty out of the tent.

Grandpa's TV was on, but he was asleep in his recliner. Liberty shook him. "Grandpa, you should go to bed."

Grandpa's eyes opened. "Is something wrong?"

"You need to go to bed."

"Speak up. I turned off my hearing aids."

Great. So much for asking where the key was. Liberty pointed to the bed.

"Oh, yeah, I should go to bed. Are you girls done already?"

Liberty shook her head. "I need the key to the well!" she said loudly.

"You broke the well?"

"I need the key to the well!"

Grandpa played with his hearing aids until they emitted a screech. "What did you say?"

"I need the key to the well."

"Nope. You are not breaking into it again."

"But we need to fix it. Last time, we accidentally dropped a spoon down the well. Stainless steel has iron in it. Makenna has this big magnet, and we hope to bring it up. If we rid the well of the iron, there won't be any more bacteria."

Grandpa frowned. "I don't trust you and your cousins with the key."

"Please?"

"I'll go get it, but I get to supervise. If you and your cousins are up to any shenanigans, I'm going to close the well until the professionals come."

"Great. Where is the key?"

"I'm not telling you that. Go down to the well, and I'll bring the key to you."

# CHAPTER 20

Sleep wouldn't come. Oliver turned on his bedside lamp. He'd been dreaming of Liberty, again. Never had a woman so completely captivated him. He checked the clock. There was no point in trying to go back to sleep. Oliver pulled on a t-shirt and sat at his desk. He'd found a source of goose quills at a bespoke clothiers shop. Apparently, people wore period clothing for events and such.

After checking the sharpness of the penknife, Oliver carved a new quill pen and opened the journal he'd purchased at Red Leaves Books. He practiced a few letters. His lettering was getting better. It was time to write something real.

From his bottom drawer, he took a piece of high cotton blend paper he'd purchased from the same shop as the quills.

*Dear Liberty—*

*I have so much to say to you. How did your reunion go? I am sure your event was a success. I keep thinking about you. You know that already because I put all my feelings in last night's letter. Not that I'll ever send the letter; it was overly sentimental.*

Oliver dipped his pen in the inkwell. What was he doing? He was not some hero from a famous British novel. He didn't know the first thing about writing letters to woo a woman.

Oliver crumpled up the paper and threw it in the dustbin with the others.

Makenna read the safety instructions for the magnet. Losing the magnet in the well would be disastrous. Eden and Claire checked the knot and the rope.

Liberty kept glancing out of the tent toward the house for Grandpa. "He was pretty tired. I hope he didn't fall back asleep."

"I haven't fallen asleep. Took a while to get the key." Grandpa held up a long steel rod with notches on the end. Dirt clung to a couple of sections.

Eden reached for the key. "Do you mind if I wash and sanitize this? We don't want anything more to contaminate the well."

Grandpa handed over the key with a grunt.

Claire hurried after Eden. "I'm coming too."

Keira found an extra bright lantern and hung it from the center of the tent. After a moment, Eden and Claire returned with the key.

Grandpa took the key and took over the operation. "I get to open the well. And if I say shut this down, we are done. Liberty, the doctor said you are still to limit how much you lift—and don't even tell me you've been wearing your sling enough. Makenna and Keira, you two are in charge of the magnet and the rope."

Liberty didn't argue. That was exactly how she would have asked her cousins to help.

Grandpa put the key in the lock and tried to turn it. Eden ended up helping him. Once it was unlocked, the two of them lifted the cover. The light from the overhead lantern only lit the first fifteen feet of the well's shaft. Makenna fed the magnet into the well. Keira had tied the end of the rope around her waist in a bowline. She also held the end of the rope in her gloved hands. The rope would not get lost down the well without taking Keira as well, who wouldn't fit in the hole.

"I think I hit bottom," said Makenna when the nylon rope went slack.

Grandpa peered over the side. "Move the magnet around a bit."

Makenna tightened and slackened the rope much too slowly for Liberty's liking.

After ten minutes, Grandpa supervised bringing the magnet up. Claire stood by with a large plastic tub. Josie held a mop handle in place on top of the well's wall so the rope slid over the handle instead of the side of the well.

When the magnet came into view, the spoon wasn't the only item clinging to it. As soon as the magnet cleared the hole, Claire slid the storage bin under the magnet. She and Eden worked to remove the spoon and other items.

Makenna picked up a rusted horseshoe. "This must be decades old."

Liberty took the horseshoe from her and dusted off the rust. "This isn't a real horseshoe. The writing says *Made in China*, copyright five years ago. It looks like the ones you can buy for home decor. The dropped spoon isn't the culprit."

"How did it get in there?" asked Dean.

Josie wiped off the magnet. "Honestly, Uncle Dean, we haven't been in the well for thirteen years."

"I know you haven't, but someone has." Dean examined his key. "And not with this key. I guess I should have replaced the extra lock when I found the old one broken last winter. With the blizzard, I put off getting it replaced quickly."

"Should we try again?" asked Keira.

Dean rubbed his jaw. "I think we should."

They repeated the process. This time the magnet came up clean.

"Hopefully, that is everything." Liberty opened the bottle of bleach.

"You're sure this is correct?" asked Keira.

Liberty bit her lip. "If I say this feels right, will you think I am crazy?"

Everyone including Dean shook their heads.

"I'm going to pour this stuff in. It needs to sit for about an hour, then I need to run the water until we can't smell anything and the water is clear."

"What if the water doesn't run clear?" asked Grandpa.

Liberty didn't like the answer she had to give, as the method could permanently harm the well. "I'll need to call a professional."

"I can pour it," offered Dean.

Liberty shook her head. "I'll hold it with my left hand. Please trust me on this."

Dean studied her for a moment. Liberty felt her worth measured and weighed by some scale she didn't understand and didn't feel adequate for. Finally, he nodded his head.

Liberty leaned over the well and poured the bleach into the hole. A splash echoed up the side of the well. When the gallon was half gone, she stopped and closed her eyes. How much was too much? What was too little? She listened for an answer or hoped for a vision like Makenna's.

Nothing.

Slowly Liberty started pouring the bleach again. Then she noticed it. The sound of the bleach hitting the water shifted not even a half tone. Liberty poured a little more. The tone grew richer sounding. She stopped. "Did you hear that? I think it is enough."

"I didn't hear anything other than a bit of splashing," said Josie, who stood nearest.

Liberty looked at Grandpa. He shrugged.

She looked back at the well. It was enough. "Now, we wait."

"No, now, I lock up the well and go to bed." Grandpa did as he said. On the way out of the tent, he paused and turned. He handed the key to Liberty. "I can trust you with this now. Put a padlock on the lid."

"I purchased one last week. I wasn't sure why I needed one. I'll be back in a minute." She took the well key from her grandfather and hurried to the shed where she'd stored the new padlock. On the way back, she stopped by the vacant chicken coop and hid the well key in the rafters. She could find a better place when it wasn't raining.

With the padlock secured, Makenna turned the bright lantern down and the cousins sat down.

Claire looked at her phone. "It was exactly midnight when you stopped pouring the bleach down the well."

Liberty checked her own phone. Somehow the time seemed significant, even if there wasn't a full moon hiding behind the clouds above the tent.

They each took turns talking about their lives and asking Eden about hers. Many of her answers were vague, but no one pressed her for answers. Liberty half listened to the other cousins' stories as she tried to puzzle out who would have deliberately tried to ruin the well.

Claire's phone chimed. "It has been an hour, should we go run the water?"

Liberty stood. "Makenna, will you turn off the lights? We can put away the tent in the morning."

"You're not worried about first-timers trying what we did?"

Liberty laughed. "I'm more worried about someone trying to put something in the well."

The water ran in the old sink for over a half hour before the water was clear. Liberty let the faucet run for fifteen minutes more before they all agreed the water didn't smell like rotten eggs anymore.

Liberty filled the old kettle. "I think this calls for some hawthorn berry tea."

# CHAPTER 21

Only two more days until Oliver could talk to Liberty. He wondered what she would think of his surprise. His mobile pinged. Mum.

— *Where are you? We need to talk.*

Oliver found his mother in the breakfast room overlooking the back garden. "What do you need, Mum?"

"I need you to stop hovering over me and get back to the States and finish whatever you started."

Oliver took a seat on the other side of the table. "Uncle Pierceton said I can oversee things from here."

"I'm not talking about one of those hotels. Every time your mobile pings, you look at the screen and frown. You aren't hoping for some hotel to call." Mum sipped from her teacup.

"But you need me."

"No, I needed you last week at the hospital when the doctor gave me results and instructions while I was on painkillers. I have a health nurse to help with my bandages— which you will never see anyway. I'll start chemo soon, and I don't want you taking care of me. There isn't much you can do. Mrs. White has been a loyal housekeeper, and she says

I couldn't fire her if I wanted to. Your father should come back soon. He will either be able to handle the changes in me or go back to London. Go talk to her. You can come back and hover in a week. But whatever is wrong, you will not solve your relationship in a text message."

Going back to Hawthorne would solve so many things. Oliver had wondered how to pull a trip to the US without hurting his mother. "You're sure you don't want me?"

"Son, I'll always want you. I just don't need you at the moment. If the chemo doesn't go well, I may need you again. But right now, you need to solve your own problems."

Oliver kissed his mother on the cheek, then drove to the office.

Uncle Pierceton frowned when Oliver told him he needed to return to Massachusetts. "I don't need you in the States right now. We are waiting for all the legal paperwork to clear. You can start on the project in Mexico."

"Then I'll take a vacation. I need to go." Oliver knew his vacation request couldn't be denied. Other than for his mother's surgery, he hadn't taken time off in months.

"Fine. One week. Your head hasn't been in the right place, anyway."

"When I get back, we need to have a long conversation about my place at Bradford-Stone. I don't think I am the person to lead this company into the next decade."

Pierceton frowned. "You're serious about these new directions?"

"We've been running inns and hotels since travelers came by post coaches. Not everyone has the innkeeper's gene. I need a chance to figure out if there is something better out there for me. I will not leave you stranded."

"I know you won't." Pierceton put a hand on Oliver's shoulder. "I should have told you earlier—you did a good job rectifying our Massachusetts situation. I'm proud of you. Have a pleasant flight."

That was the most praise Oliver had received in his years with the company. Likely, he wouldn't receive any more for another decade. "See you in a week."

Oliver stopped to give directions to his office manager before hurrying home to pack.

As the clock struck noon, Liberty checked the last of the reunion guests out. Most had left on Monday, but a handful waited until today. She'd hired extra help through a temp agency to help with the extra cleaning.

The front door opened, and Eden entered.

"I thought you'd left."

Eden took a brown glass jar out of her bag. "I'm on my way to the airport. I made you a new salve for your rash."

Liberty lifted her sleeve and rotated her arm to show Eden the rash. "I rinsed my arm in well water this morning. It's less red, but it still itches."

"I took a cup of the water with me Sunday night—early Monday morning—when I left. I used the water in this. If I guessed right, the well water may give this salve some extra healing power." Eden opened the jar. Liberty couldn't identify the smell beyond the comforting feeling that swirled around her.

Liberty dipped her finger in and rubbed some on her arm. The cooling effect was immediate. "Wow. That is amazing." Liberty checked in the mirror she kept behind the desk. The red rash was calming much faster than with water alone. "Thanks, Eden."

"You're welcome."

"Come back soon. If you ever need a place to stay, I'll have a room here for you."

"I just might." Eden waved as she closed the door behind her.

Something crashed in the kitchen. Liberty rushed through the door. Fiona stood over the remains of multiple glass jars full of custom herbal tea blends. "Sorry. I dropped them."

Only one of the jars contained hawthorn berries. The other two were apple spice tea blends she'd made last fall. "You dropped them? What were you doing with them? You clocked out an hour ago."

"I needed to move them." Fiona disappeared into the open janitorial closet.

Liberty had never fired someone before. She wasn't even sure she could. But this couldn't have been an accident. Before firing Fiona, she should talk to Mom and Grandpa.

Liberty went back to dealing with the books. An email came in through the online reservation system. Mr. Imus Dupp reserved room six from the 21st through the 28th. Liberty entered the reservation into the system. There were only seven other reservations, and only one had requested a specific room. Liberty brought up last year's reservations for the last week of April. They'd only had six rooms filled. Maybe her mom's website was directing more traffic.

The cook came through the employee door behind the desk carrying a paper. "This is my resignation. You served your terrible secret tea the last two days. I told you, I was to be in charge of everything. You are stifling my creative abilities."

"You're quitting over tea?" One explanation for the broken bottles.

"And all the nosey ladies who came into the kitchen this last week, thinking that being a Covington relative gave them the right to be there. All asking why I thinned down the maple syrup or why there was quiche instead of corned beef hash. If I wanted to be a fry cook, I would have applied to one of those chain restaurants."

"You had several restaurants on your resume." The experience at the food chains had been part of the reason they'd hired her.

The woman huffed and took off her apron. "Forget the two-week notice—I'm leaving now!"

The cook marched out the front door, slamming it behind her.

Lisa's laughter came from the top of the stairs and grew as she descended.

"Mom?"

"I'm glad she is gone. Fiona's been so difficult. I knew you hired her to free up my time, but we don't need her. Watching her this last week, I picked up some tricks for being more efficient. Besides, I miss interacting with the guests and the compliments, rather than fielding complaints about the cooking not being up to par."

"I'll admit, we had more complaints about the food this past month. No one said it was bad, it just wasn't yours." Opening the file drawer, Liberty slipped the resignation into the employee file.

"I'm glad we had her while your shoulder was mending and for the reunion. I don't think we could have gotten everything done otherwise."

"Do you suppose I'll remember in thirteen years that being on the committee isn't such a good thing?"

"Not a chance. If Grandma Tansy walked in that door tomorrow and asked you to chair the committee, you would."

"Nope. No way. Not happening. I can't keep saying yes to everything." Liberty touched her right shoulder. "If I learned anything this month, it is that I can't plan on doing it all. And it is okay to say no."

"Instead of a cook, I thought we might hire a couple of part-timers to help with the rooms. I love to do the cooking but not the toilets."

"I think I can put that in the budget now that we don't have to pay a cook."

Grandpa came in carrying the mail. "That nephew of mine has secured himself a lawyer. Well, I'll tell you what I'm going to do. I already called my attorney. He can see us at three. Liberty, you'd better be ready to come with me. I'm signing the B&B over to you. I can't find one shred of anything saying I can't. Male, female, married, single—I've even searched the internet. I own this place free and clear, and I can do anything I want to with it. And since I can trust you with the well key, I can trust you with the whole place."

"Great, so now Clifton will try to sue me?"

"Not a chance. I'll get our lawyer to talk to his lawyer." Grandpa chuckled. "Listen to me. Not even retired yet, and I sound all highfalutin."

"You aren't going to stop working, are you?"

"As long as I live here, I'll help here. You aren't kicking me out, are you?"

Liberty threw her arms around Grandpa and hugged him. "Never."

# CHAPTER 22

The ride share driver pulled into the parking lot of Covington House Bed & Breakfast. Finally. After nine hours in a plane, and then ninety minutes with a chatty driver, Oliver was here. He took a deep breath, not knowing what kind of reception he'd get when he walked through the door. Would Liberty like the ideas he was implementing, or would she still be upset with him? These were the same questions he'd asked all the way over the Atlantic and still couldn't answer.

He counted to three and opened the door.

"What are you doing here?" Liberty's face registered shock, not anger.

A hint of a smile on Liberty's lips gave Oliver confidence to flirt. "Strange, you asked that same question last time I came to check in."

Liberty looked at the computer screen. "You don't have reservations."

"Sure, I do. They are under Mr. Imus Dupp. I've been pretty stupid, and I figured if I used that name, you might let me stay long enough to at least talk."

Her eyes widened. "You booked the room for eight nights."

Oliver leaned over the desk and lowered his voice. "I'm hoping you want to talk for a very long time."

A blush rose in her cheeks. Liberty turned to the key wall. Her hand hovered over the box for number six for a moment too long. When she turned back, the blush remained, yet her expression was all business. "I am working until six. Here is your key. Enjoy your stay."

Oliver pulled an envelope out of his pocket and flipped it over twice. The ink on the front had only smeared in one place. He tapped it on the desk twice. Last night, writing the letter seemed like such a good idea. Facing her he wasn't sure if he was right or wrong. There was something oddly romantic about using this newly found obsession with quill pens to write to her. He handed the letter to Liberty and hurried up the stairs before she could glare at him.

Liberty counted the steps overhead and waited until Oliver was at his room before she reacted, covering her mouth to not scream. He was here. And he wanted to talk. He'd even written her a letter with inkblots. Judging by the amount of ink on his right ring finger, a pen had exploded during the process.

There wasn't a chance in the world she was going to get any meaningful work done in the next three hours with the knowledge that he was upstairs. He looked so happy. He must not realize she'd learned about the sale. Frankly, she hadn't thought about the property much in the last few days—one advantage of being crazy busy with the reunion. Last time they'd talked—or she yelled—she hadn't given him a chance to explain.

The letter sat in the center of the registration desk. To open or not to open? He obviously wanted her to read it before they talked. Yet if she became emotional at the front desk…

From their few texts, she assumed she'd get a text, email, or even a phone call today. But face-to-face and a letter? Yikes.

Keira couldn't bake enough calming cookies to help with this unexpected meeting, never mind how Liberty's heart thudded like a happy puppy's tail when Oliver had come through the door.

Liberty texted her cousins' group chat. *OLIVER IS HERE! (Sorry for shouting.)*

*Makenna: What?*

*Claire: I thought I saw him in the back of a car 10 minutes ago. But I told myself it couldn't be him.*

*Josie: Do you need more chocolate?*

*Eden: Is this the guy that builds hotels?*

*Keira: I made a new recipe. A strawberry jam tart with the calming effect of the cookies, but it seems to… it's hard to explain. I tested the tarts on my regulars. The old men who play games in the corner of the cafe haven't grumbled all morning, even Walter, and they are more insightful than usual.*

*Liberty: I think I need a dozen of them.*

*Keira: I only have 3 left.*

*Liberty. 2 for me and 1 for Oliver?*

*Makenna: Walter not grumbling? I'll get him to cover the store and deliver the cookies. And yes, Eden, this is the hotel guy… From England!*

*Josie: Makenna, come by and grab some chocolate in case she needs it.*

*Claire: Have you spoken with him?*

*Liberty: I checked him in a few minutes ago and said we could talk when my work was over. He reserved the room under the name.* Mr. Imus Dupp. *I messed up! It sounds better in his accent. What am I going to do? I want to run upstairs and see him and I want to go hide!?!?*

*Eden: Did he use a company card or a personal one?*

*Liberty: I'll look.*

*Makenna: Walter is here, he is in a good mood. Those tarts do something.*

*Liberty: The card isn't the same number he used before.*
*Josie: I bet he used his personal card. That means he is here for you.*
*Liberty: EEEK. I don't know what to do.*
*Claire: Be calm and listen. You told us that was what you wanted to do when you spoke to him. Remember, there could be some explanation for what Trina told you.*
*Eden: Drink some of your hawthorn berry tea with the good water. It probably won't fix anything, but it is something your body is used to.*
*Liberty: Like comfort food?*
*Josie: Still sending chocolate.*

After setting the *Ring bell for service* sign on the desk, Liberty hurried into the kitchen.

*Claire: Do you want things to work out with Oliver?*

That was the big question. As much as Liberty had tried to keep him out of her thoughts during the busy weekend, he'd always been lurking—along with sadness that he was gone.

*Liberty: I always knew this would be a short-term romance. All I can hope for is that when it ends, we are still friends.*
*Josie: I don't see why you don't figure out a way to make it work.*
*Liberty: I'm not giving up the B&B and he isn't going to stop being VP of his company. This can't last long-term.*
*Claire: What if he is more important than the B&B?*

No one else typed. Liberty knew they were waiting for her.
*Liberty: I don't know. I need to go now. Later…*

She looked at the letter. The 'T' in her name was smudged. Almost the same way Oliver said her name with a soft 'T' rather than a harsh one. She wasn't sure why she hadn't told her cousins about it. Makenna would be here in minutes.

The old letter opener sliced through the envelope. Liberty looked around and checked the one camera in the parking lot before she unfolded the paper. The lettering wasn't even and in places there were ink dots, as if Oliver used a pen that leaked.

Dear Liberty—

I've wanted to speak with you for several days. Not about hotels, or about land or work. Just talk to you. About life, about my mom's surgery, about my absentee father, about the rainstorm this morning, about the comedy show I saw. About nothing, and about everything.

I'm afraid to fly to the States because you may still be upset with me. But I am more afraid to stay here and wonder what could have been. I'm afraid you'll give me one of those withering glares. (If Lavinia used that look on Captain Pitt, he would have surrendered and never tried to march to Concord.) Yet I hope you will smile.

I know we have things to discuss. I have a surprise for you—one that could keep me in the States, at least for part of the year. And there are other options for us to explore. This Brit doesn't want to return to England because he found a reason to stay.

There must be a way that we can find a place for us.

Hopefully yours,

Oliver

Makenna and those calming, mind-clearing tarts couldn't get there fast enough.

# CHAPTER 23

The hour nap had been refreshing but not nearly long enough. Oliver had nothing to do other than wait for the time to pass so he could speak to Liberty when her shift was over. His favorite game on his phone wasn't even helping as it kept popping up ads since he arrived in the States.

Someone walked down the hall, stopping outside his door. Oliver stopped playing his game to listen. He wasn't sure how he knew the person outside the door wasn't Liberty, Dean, or Lisa. After several long seconds, someone knocked.

Oliver had never spoken to Grandma Tansy in person, but he'd seen her often enough to recognize her.

"Aren't you going to invite me in? I won't compromise your virtue if you're worried about that." Grandma Tansy pushed past him and sat in the chair by the window. "You chose this room? Surprising since the decor celebrates your ancestor's defeat."

"How did you know I am related to Willoughby Pitt?"

"I wasn't talking about him. I meant King George III. But that is not why I am here."

Oliver sat in the desk chair. "Why are you here?"

"To find out why you are here."

He'd learned enough from Liberty and Makenna to know that Grandma Tansy didn't always make sense. Apparently, this circular conversation was part of that. However, he wouldn't offend any of Liberty's relatives. "Liberty and I had a misunderstanding that I need to clear up."

"Isn't that what telephones are for? You can call, chat, email, video, whatever. You don't need to clear things up in person."

"This is too important to leave to chance."

Grandma Tansy pursed her lips and studied him. After he sat for what seemed like an hour though it was only seconds, she spoke, "You'll do. But I don't like complications."

"I'll do? What?"

"The right thing, obviously." Grandma Tansy stood and went to the door. "Don't mention to Liberty that I came. She'll only worry."

Oliver barely made it to the door in time to open it for Grandma Tansy's exit. He wasn't sure, but the thought that he'd passed a test wouldn't leave his mind. Why would Liberty's aunt need to approve of him?

Even if Keira's new recipe didn't have any magic effects, the tart was so delicious she ate a second. Liberty pondered how she would give Oliver his before they spoke. But giving the possibly magic tart to him without informing him of the possible effects seemed like a breach of ethics. She'd read the letter again after eating the tart. Was Oliver asking her for a permanent relationship? She read the letter a third time to be sure.

Sweet hawthorn berry tea.

If he could be here part of the time, could she go to England? Would their children be British or American? Liberty shook her head to clear out the runaway thoughts. Marriage was a whole other step. And there was the B&B. If she had to choose, could she give the B&B up? The idea scared her. Could she have both? Liberty doodled on a legal pad as she pondered.

Grandpa came through the front door with a large envelope in hand.

Embarrassed for Grandpa to see the page filled with hearts, flowers, and Oliver's name, Liberty flipped the pad over. Apparently her subconscious understood what she needed.

"I went down to the county offices." He handed Liberty the envelope. "The new deed is all signed and sealed. Covington House now officially belongs to the Dean Covington Family Trust."

"The attorney's idea to set the B&B up in the trust solves so many problems." No one could argue Grandpa's will with the trust in place, and no one person was responsible to make all the business decisions now.

"I added your mother to the trust. She may not have been born here, but she should be a part of this too."

"When are you going to tell her?"

Grandpa tucked the papers back into the envelope. "I told her this morning. And as I expected, she broke down in tears. You women and your crying. I'll go put this away and be down to take my turn at the desk. I understand you have plans for the evening."

"How do you know that?" asked Liberty.

"I saw Mr. Imus Dupp on the reservation list. Figured Mr. *I-messed-up* was flying over from England to give you an apology. Who else would use the pseudonym?"

"How did you get that from his name?"

Dean shrugged and exited through the employee door. Liberty ripped the page off of the legal pad and ran it through the shredder, not wanting to leave evidence that she was willing to choose Oliver over her home if she had to.

Oliver came down the stairs. The sweater over the button-down didn't look dorky on him at all. "Still working?"

"Grandpa will be here in a moment. Would you like a tart? They're Keira's newest creation."

He picked it up.

Just as he was about to take a bite, Liberty yelled, "Stop!"

Oliver lowered his hand.

"You can't eat that without knowing the tart might be magic."

"What does this one do—or what is it *supposed* to do?"

"Keira thinks the tart works like the calming cookies, only it makes conversations better because people think more. I ate one, but I thought you should know before you did."

Oliver set the tart back on the napkin. "I may eat it later, but I want you to know that anything I do or say is all me. No magic or possible magical interference."

"I should have thought of that before I ate one or two." Liberty felt calmer, even though the fast-wagging puppy had taken over her heart again.

"No brace. Does that mean you can drive? There is something I want to explain and show you at the same time."

"I'm good to drive. Although I am under strict instructions not to get in an accident." Liberty stood and scooted the chair under the desk.

"Excellent advice."

Dean came out of the kitchen area. "Evening, Oliver. Take care of my girl tonight, and watch where you are driving."

"Liberty is driving. The rental car company wanted a huge deposit on a beat-up car from the '90s."

Dean tossed his head back and laughed.

"Night, Grandpa." Liberty handed off the master keychain. "Oliver, do you mind waiting while I go change into a sweater?"

Liberty changed quickly, adding some make-up but not so much her lip-gloss would smear if they kissed—*when* they kissed. She hadn't realized how much she'd missed his smile, his voice, and just … him. Determined to work out everything from international relationships to the property in Weston, she grabbed the keys to the car and hurried to find Oliver waiting in the lobby.

"I considered giving you crazy directions to get to our destination, but I realized you probably wouldn't get turned around and lost like I was. So will you drive to the warehouse in Weston?" asked Oliver.

Liberty pinched her lips. "You're sure. Last time we were there… our conversation didn't go well. Especially my part."

"My explanation will make more sense at the warehouse."

"Okay." Liberty drove, her face passive. Oliver had never seen her expression so blank.

As they got near, Oliver started talking. "When I was looking for properties to suggest to my uncle, I came here twice. Both times, my driver drove from other places we'd looked at, and both times I didn't go back to Covington House. Until I followed you through the woods and fields, I didn't realize how close this place was to yours. It takes nearly five miles to drive, so I'd assumed the location was further than the one in Concord that I didn't suggest."

"Your text said they were building in Cambridge."

"They are. The property is tourist-friendly." Oliver's statement didn't even raise one of Liberty's eyebrows.

"I was told Bradford bought the property. Why are you building here too?"

"I'm not building here, but I bought the property."

Her eyes widened in curiosity. Liberty turned into the driveway and parked in the center of the asphalt lot. "Why, if you aren't building a hotel?"

"I bought the property. Not Bradford-Stone."

Liberty turned to look at him, seemingly willing to listen.

"Remember when we discussed a co-op for bed and breakfasts? I couldn't find one in the area. So, I'm creating one. I'll spare you the technical details. In short, I need a warehouse. This one is centrally located to B&Bs all over New England—and no one can build a competing hotel on the land in the future while I own it."

"I thought… I mean, I ran into a real estate agent who said you'd purchased this place right after you texted me. I thought you'd lied."

"I never dreamed you'd find out about this purchase. I wish you had asked."

"I was so busy with the reunion. Every time I started to text, someone or something interrupted me. Apparently, the intervention was a good thing so I didn't fly off the handle again." Liberty giggled. "Keira's tarts must do something. It shocked me when you asked me to come here. I don't think I would have been so calm. After your letter, my heart was racing so fast. You do something dangerous to my insides."

Oliver fought to keep a straight face. Her admission that he was causing her heart to palpitate the same way his did around her made his own heart beat faster. "So you only listened because of the tarts?"

"No, I already decided I would listen. I just probably would have given you an earful on the drive over. I thought about all the words, but then I realized I needed more information—a realization I've known for days."

"So her tarts prevent fights?"

"Maybe. Or maybe they are like counting to ten before

you speak and not jumping to conclusions." Liberty leaned against the boot of the car. "So what does that mean for you, starting a new company?"

"I'm not sure. I am not happy in the family business, but that may just be because my uncle and my father don't get on. I'm still trying to figure that out."

"Oh, I didn't ask—how is your mother?"

"She is doing well. In fact, she told me to stop hovering and fly over here."

"Do you think you'll stay in the States?"

"I don't know if I can. But if I have a good reason to stay..."

"I'm thinking of getting a passport. Maybe I should go see England."

"If you come to Leeds, my mother has more than enough rooms to put you up. But can you leave the B&B?"

"November, most of December, and January through Mid-April are slower months. I might hire someone to take my place for now."

"What about later?"

"Grandpa put it into a trust with him, my mom, and me. From April through October, I need to be here, but maybe not the slow months." Liberty shrugged.

"Most bed and breakfasts in the area would have the same slow months, I'm assuming?"

"Probably. Except the few inside the 95 closest to Boston. Tourists keep those full year-round."

"We do most of our hotel planning in the winter months. I usually get July and August off. April to June, I spend going to hotels and scaring managers into cleaning the place up. If I were to work exclusively in North and South America I could be based in Boston." Just one of his options if he stayed with Bradford-Stone.

"Did we just figure out how to make a two-country relationship work?" asked Liberty.

"I think we did. Do you want to give it a go?"

"A go?"

"See if we can make this into something permanent?"

Liberty ran her hands up Oliver's chest and around his neck. "On one condition. I am the primary driver in the States, and you can drive in the UK."

"And Australia." He kissed her on the nose.

"And New Zealand." Oliver ran a string of kisses down her jaw.

"And South Africa."

"Just shut up and really kiss me." Liberty pulled his head down to meet hers.

Some way, this would work, providing Liberty still agreed when the tart wore off.

Liberty ended the kiss. "Do you know I've never been outside of the New England states? This could be a new adventure."

"I hope our adventure is a very long one." Oliver pulled her close and kissed her again, thankful he'd won over this American by losing his heart.

# Epilogue

The Independence Day reenactment was unusual in that it didn't depict a particular battle. Instead the historical play featured notable Massachusetts patriots from across the entire panorama of the Revolutionary War. The format was Liberty's favorite. The show started with William Dawes's ride to warn the minutemen of the approach of the redcoats.

Over a loudspeaker, narrators explained the significance of each event to onlookers, from the Battles of Lexington and Concord, to lesser-known battles fought in New York State and further south. As the sun inched toward its zenith, the tent where Liberty waited to play the role of Deborah Sampson grew warm. Finally, the time came for her to follow Captain Webb onto the field for the battle where she would be shot and wounded, but her alias not discovered. All eyes would be on Liberty as the narrators told the story of the woman who disguised herself as a man and fought for the last seventeen months of the Revolutionary War.

The scene director gave the signal for the Deborah Sampson story. Liberty reached her mark closest to the audience and raised her hat so they would know that she was the female they were to watch as her regiment advanced on the British troops.

Something was wrong. The redcoat reenactors were not on their marks. A British general flanked by two junior officers, one carrying a white flag, advanced across the field. Liberty looked to the reenactor next to her and whispered, "What is going on?"

The reenactor shrugged.

"Halt!" The man playing the role of the American Captain held up his arm. Liberty and the others stood in place.

Silence swept over the field as the narrator stopped speaking, and the crowd grew quiet.

In perfect marching step, the British general continued across the field until he reached the American captain.

The Captain turned to face his men. "Robert Shurtliff! Report!"

The alias name of Deborah Sampson wasn't supposed to be called. Liberty froze. The reenactor behind her gave her a push. The one next to her snickered.

A squeak came from the loudspeakers as the narrator started speaking, but not the script that Liberty and the others had practiced. "On, July 3, 1782 near Tarrytown, New York, Deborah took two musket balls in her thigh and sustained a cut on her forehead. Before a surgeon could treat her, she fled from the hospital where she removed one ball herself and carried the other with her until her death. They did not discover her true identity that day. However, folks, we will not see the event in today's reenactment."

Liberty reached the captain and the redcoats. The General was not any reenactor she'd ever seen before, instead it was Oliver. He was supposed to be in England. They'd talked last night about the success of the co-op and Oliver's plans to expand them. She just purchased tickets to surprise him in Leeds next week. Her steps faltered as she reported to her captain. Her heartbeat kicked up a notch as it always did when she saw him.

The surrounding reenactors stood at ease smiling. Actors playing the parts of the Americans and the two British soldiers stepped back, leaving her to face Oliver alone.

"Ladies and Gents, Patriots and foes. On the field we have Liberty Belle Covington playing the role of Deborah. Liberty is a long-time reenactor for the Hawthorn Volunteers and is the direct descendant of Lavinia Hawthorne Covington who, according to legend, stopped an entire regiment of redcoats from reaching Concord in 1775. The General is played by Oliver Bradford, who is a descendant of King George III and the fifth cousin twice removed to the current British monarch. What we are witnessing now is not a reenactment."

A hush fell over the field. Oliver removed his hat and knelt on one knee in front of Liberty. Tears filled her eyes and her throat swelled. Oliver was here, kneeling. Her passport only arrived yesterday. Did he know she was planning on going to England next week?

"Liberty Belle Covington, you have captured me, body and soul. I returned to my ancestral home in England only to discover it's not a home at all because you are not there. I surrender all I have to you, even my accent, if you will have me forever. Please marry me?" Oliver opened his palm to reveal a princess cut diamond flanked by a ruby and a blue tanzanite set on a platinum band. Red, white, and blue, the colors of both of their countries.

She tried to speak. After two attempts, a faint yes passed her lips. At Oliver's smile she shouted louder so everyone could hear. The reenactors on the field and the audience on the sidelines cheered. Oliver stood and dropped Liberty's hat to the ground. Liberty wrapped her arms around his neck and kissed him hard. There would be no misunderstanding. Liberty pulled back. "I received my passport."

"Good. Mum would murder me if we don't visit occasionally."

"You'll live here?"

"Always."

# Acknowledgments

I can't possibly thank everyone who helped me get this book completed and out, as the list includes most of my Facebook friends list. Maria thank you for being understanding and including me in this magical journey. Jenny thank you for the sprints and the kick start.

As always, thanks to Tammy, Nanette, Julie, and Cami who are so willing to help make all my projects better and to read for all my mistakes. I would never make it through a day without Nichole, Sally and Cindy whose advice keeps me going. Thank you wonderful ladies.

Thank you to my excellent co-writer for sharing her editing ability. And to my excellent proofreaders who are not to be to be blamed for any remaining errors. Thank you all!

My family, for sharing their home with the fictional characters who often get fed better than they did. And my husband who encourages me every crazy step of the way and puts up with all my messy spreadsheets.

And to my Father in Heaven for putting these wonderful people, and any I may have forgotten to mention, in my life. I am grateful for every experience and blessing I have been granted.

# ABOUT THE AUTHORS

*L*orin Grace was born in Colorado and has been moving around the country ever since, living in eight states and several imaginary worlds. She holds a degree in graphic design which comes in handy with creating book covers. Currently, she lives with her husband, and a dog who is insanely jealous of her laptop. When not writing, Lorin enjoys creating graphics, visiting historical sites, museums, painting furniture, and reading. Three of her books, her debut novel, *Waking Lucy* (2017), *Mending Fences* (2018), and *Not the Bodyguard's Baby* (2020) have won Recommend Read awards in the League of Utah Writers Published book contest.

*W*hen Maria Hoagland is not working at her computer, she can be found combing used furniture stores and remodeling houses with her husband. She loves crunching leaves in the fall, stealing cookie dough from the mixing bowl, and listening to musicals on her phone. Maria has several published works in the sweet romance and women's fiction genres. Two of her books, *Still Time* and *The ReModel Marriage* have been Whitney Award finalists.

www.ingramcontent.com/pod-product-compliance
Lightning Source LLC
Chambersburg PA
CBHW070020260626
47159CB00005B/1898